Teen Spies

Teen Spies

WARTIME CHARLOTTESVILLE SLEUTHS

JIM SARGENT AND AUDREY DEICHMANN

Published by Jim Sargent
https://www.jimsargentbooks.com/

Cover by Fiona Jayde Media
Layout design by Christianna Deichmann

Paperback ISBN: 979-8-9931090-0-8

ePub ISBN: 979-8-9931090-1-5

Library of Congress Control Number: 2024911223

Dedication

For the ones who came before us, the ones who walk beside us, and the ones who will carry the torch next.

This book was dreamed up across three generations: from father to daughter to granddaughter.

May it inspire young hearts to believe in their stories—and in each other.

With love,

From our family to yours.

CHAPTER 1
Charlottesville in the War Years

Late in the afternoon I found myself driving our father's old black '36 Chevy pickup slowly along the narrow mountain road and hitting every rut from here to tomorrow. Calling it a *road* might be an exaggeration. The gravel and dirt lanes were barely wide enough for two vehicles to pass. Overhead the sky was a brilliant blue. On the left I saw a thick forest of tall trees, like oaks, chestnuts, and maples surrounded by leafy bushes everywhere. To the right there weren't as many trees or bushes, and the land sloped downward.

Drops of sweat slipped through my eyebrows as I kept scanning the trees for a hidden cabin. I couldn't have been driving fifteen miles an hour when I spotted a lane on the right leading into the woods. I braked so hard the engine stalled. I tried to start it, but no dice. The six-cylinder engine rolled over, coughed, and faded to nothing. I had both windows rolled down. Listening carefully, I heard nothing but silence.

A buck with a big rack appeared from behind a towering oak. Stepping boldly into the road a few yards ahead of me, the deer stared at me with its coal black eyes. I had Dad's S&W revolver with me, but I couldn't risk firing a shot. It might give me away. I poked my head out the side window and yelled, *"Get outta here!"*

The buck glared at me like I was the enemy. Another idea hit me. Hanging my arm out the window, I banged the door twice, really hard. Instantly the buck wheeled and vanished into the trees. Smiling, I tried to start the engine again. It sputtered, and then came to life. I listened to the grumble of the motor.

I figured to drive a little further and get the lay of the land. Shifting into first, I motored slowly ahead. In a couple hundred yards I rounded a bend, and I saw an old log store with a gas pump in front, a few parking spaces beside it, and a wooden sign overhead. Next to the old store sat a black Ford Model A pickup with big headlamps protruding like a pair of owl eyes.

Pushing open the driver's door to get out, I put my left foot down on the running board when I heard a loud *Bang*. Opening my eyes, I sat up in bed. "Oh, Geez, more dreaming," I said quietly.

Every time I dream about our spy affair of a year ago, I wake up in a cold sweat. Actually, I'm lucky to be alive, let alone be able to sweat. My sister and I came so close to death that I still have nightmares. We had to escape two German agents, but perhaps more importantly, we had to make certain they would never again threaten us.

Afterward, we told a sanitized version to our father and the FBI, but we kept the harsh reality a secret. Sometime later on, when I have a typewriter and learn to type, I will convert this handwritten manuscript into a typed document and store it in a safe place. If something unpredictable happens, the truth will find a niche in history.

Sitting there, I heard the distinctive *chirr* of a robin from my open window. Rubbing my eyes, I realized the robin's appearance was uncanny. I glared at the feathered intruder. When that didn't work, I growled in my best Bogey accent, "Of all the open windows on all the farms in the world, you have to land on my windowsill; and on this very day, of all the days of the year …"

Exactly one year earlier, a similar bird on the same windowsill had awakened me with its call. Later that morning, my sister and I had embarked on our teen spy adventure. I reflected on whether today's robin was the same bird from a year ago. It seemed unlikely, given all the stray cats roaming the neighborhood.

Gazing out the window at our faded red barn, the rows of apple trees stretching out behind our buildings, and the brilliant azure sky framing the scene; I let my mind drift back to that memorable morning in May of 1942. At that time World War II seemed like a distant cloud on the horizon. But I knew boys just a few years older than me and my friends were training to fight in Europe against the Germans and their sidekicks the Italians, and in the Pacific against the Japanese.

One year ago, I remember flipping back the bed covers, sitting up, and yawning. The bedroom window shade was halfway up, and the bright sun looked in at me like a burning orange eye. The alarm clock said 7:01. Sighing, I remembered it was Saturday, and school in Charlottesville wouldn't let out for the year for another week. Summer vacation sure changed life on the farm.

Even so, Saturday was Dad's favorite day. He knew he could depend on getting plenty of work out of me and Natalia, or Nat, as we called my sister. We lived on our family's farm a half mile south of town. Occasionally I wondered if Thomas Jefferson had ever come out our way. Actually, I believe he had when making the rounds of the land spread out from his home, Monticello, up there on his own hill.

Forgetting Jefferson, I climbed out of bed. Pulling on a white tee shirt and my Levis, I laced up my brown shoes. The toe on the left shoe was darn near worn out, but with the war going on, we were told it was our patriotic duty to make clothes and shoes last as long as possible because so many kinds of raw materials were going into the war effort. Anyway, I just wear these shoes for chores. I wear my good black shoes for school and church.

Looking around, my eyes landed on the framed black-and-white portrait of our mother and father taken on their wedding day in 1927. It had that sepia look you see in many old pictures. Dad hung it next to the dark wooden dresser, the one Uncle Matthew made. He earned his living as a carpenter, but in his spare time, he made furniture before he passed away.

Looking in the oval mirror on the dresser, I smiled at the slender, nice-looking guy with the wide blue eyes, thin nose, and short brown hair. Of course, my hair could use a *little* combing. I frowned, and the mirror frowned back. I winked at the reflection, and it winked back.

I thought *Here I am, fifteen, nearly six feet tall, and almost through the 10th grade at Jefferson High. Maybe by next fall when I start the 11th grade, the girls will see me as handsome as the next Clark Gable or Cary Grant.*

Again I looked at the wedding picture of our mother and father. He was a good-looking guy, and tall at six-one. She was quite pretty and about the right height, five-two. Looking at her image, I thought she was just right in every way. Still, seeing that old picture made me feel sad.

Five years ago, on July 5, 1937, a date stuck in my memory like an anchor, a drunk driver hit our mother and killed her. The driver's name was Henry Teuton. In court he said he was sorry, but he went to prison anyway. Maybe he felt guilty, but I didn't get over the sad feeling for quite a long time. A few months later, Dad asked Aunt Cora, Mom's older sister, to come and live with us. Dad felt like she would be a real good friend, someone who would share our lives. Different, you know, but good.

Thinking about Aunt Cora, my stomach growled. *Hun-gry*, that's me! I practically flew down those wooden stairs two at a time, heading lickety-split for the smell of breakfast. When I walked in our large bright kitchen with the long white table, I saw Aunt Cora hovering in front of the stove, spatula in hand. She was frying eggs and bacon in the big black skillet. The bacon sizzled, and the smell oozed past me like an invisible cloud. My mouth started *watering*.

She looked at me, and smiled, that friendly, sweet smile of hers. Actually, Aunt Cora looks a lot like Mom. She has the same brown hair, but styled shorter, and the same brown eyes, maybe wider, and the nice nose, and thin lips. Maybe she's an inch taller, a tad thinner, and, of course, not as experienced at being a mother. Her husband Joseph Raleigh, or Uncle Joe, died of pneumonia six years ago. I heard they didn't get him to the hospital in time, but Dad never talks about it.

Anyway, Joseph and Cora never had any children. He always seemed to be busy with his jewelry and watch repair shop in Richmond. Uncle Joe was quite the craftsman, our father used to say. Anyway, Dad said we were helping Mom's sister. Of course, Aunt Cora was helping us too.

She's a good cook, that's for sure. She bakes those fluffy biscuits that *melt* in your mouth! Plus she can fry bacon, ham, and eggs, and, well, you name it.

And Nat was always helping her. In fact, my sister just finished setting the table. When I first saw her, she was smoothing our blue checked tablecloth, the one we used during the week. My sister liked it to be *real smooth*.

You know, Nat always beats me out of bed in the morning. I can't figure it out. I looked at her again. Seeing me, she grinned. She gave me a second look, glanced at Aunt Cora, and looked at me again, and then I got that slow wink. That meant she had a secret. She liked writing the private stuff in her diary every day. I grinned, because I could hardly wait to hear about it.

Nat was wearing her favorite blue blouse along with her old Levis, the ones with the right side pocket wearing out. Over her jeans she was wearing one of Mom's aprons, the one with the two red hearts on the pocket.

Nat took down the china plates from the cupboard. Aunt Cora had finished the eggs, and she was almost done with the bacon. Nat was making toast, and I was thinking maybe I'd rib her about that pocket. But I held up. It might be smarter to eat breakfast first. There's a time and a place, I always say.

I looked around our kitchen. I thought our white Victorian was a nice house, especially with the five bedrooms upstairs. That way a guy's got a little privacy. Across from Nat's room we had the spare bedroom for Aunt Cora. Like the other four bedrooms, hers had a double bed, an armchair, and another of Uncle Matthew's dressers with an oval mirror. Dad slept in the master bedroom, the biggest one, which was across from mine. Next to his, was the smaller spare bedroom usually used by guests.

Walking to the back door, I looked out at our large back yard. Glancing around, I sneaked a look at my sister. She had Mom's oval face, fair skin, and pleasant voice, but Natalia's green eyes carried a hint of brown. A year younger than me, Nat looked a bit pale, mainly because of spending most of her time inside. After Mom died, my sister handled the cooking, cleaning, and tidying up, at least until Aunt Cora came to stay. She took over the cooking and part of the cleaning, mainly downstairs.

Dad was reading the *Albemarle Gazette*. He usually sat at the far end of the table in one of our slat back chairs. He liked reading the paper while sipping coffee. It gave him a break, because he got up with the birds like the robins so he could start the day's work. Zebulon, or Zeke, as his friends called him, was forty-two, three years older than our mother.

He looked more like an athlete than a farmer. Back in the 1920s, he used to be an all-around ballplayer in Charlottesville. Of course, he grew up on a farm, so he had just enough spare time for baseball on the summer town team. Our friends liked telling stories about Dad. They said he was a hard-throwing right-hander with a wide bending curve ball. He could also slug the ball like Babe Ruth. Dad mainly smiles and doesn't say much when his friends remember those days. I got the impression he was the big star, but our father is not much for blowing his own horn. I hope to grow up and be just like him. I'm sure my brown hair and blue eyes came from him, but I'm a lefty. I never saw left-handed batters as a kid, so I batted right-handed.

Moving over to the table, I sat at the other end where Mom used to sit. You might say I inherited the place after she was gone. I could see war news about the Pacific on the back side of Dad's newspaper. Everyone knew about the terrible Japanese attack on American bases at Pearl Harbor in Hawaii on Sunday, December 7, 1941. The next day President Franklin Roosevelt gave a speech asking Congress to declare war on Japan. Boy, everyone was angry! I sure thought the President's voice sounded angry too.

Congress voted for war the same day. Mister Brontson, our Social Studies teacher, brought in newspaper clippings about the surprise attack, and he kept bringing us stories about the war.

On the evening of Tuesday, December 9, President Roosevelt gave another one of his "fireside chats" over the radio. I remember that we sat around the living room and listened while he told us how the "gangster" countries like Germany and Italy were fighting along with Japan, and all of them saw us Americans as the enemy. I remember Mister Bronston saying the Germans declared war on us on December 11. He brought in newspaper stories about that, too.

When Germany declared war on us on December 11, most of our teachers got upset all over again. Dad wouldn't say much about it. Miss Richards, who teaches English, told my class about her son Herbert. He's was in the Navy, and serving on one of those ships stationed at Pearl Harbor, the battleship *Arizona*. She found out that Herbert was one of the sailors missing in action. I don't think she ever learned what happened to him.

Nat and I happened to be talking about summer stuff while we walked home from school one day that week. It started when she mentioned working two hours, two days a week last summer at Otto Herman's house. He owned a white Victorian like ours. She said he wanted her to work three afternoons a week, once school ended for the summer. Nat had been cleaning for Otto for two summers now. She helped with our chores first, so the idea of working for him wasn't new.

My sister helping the neighbor got me to thinking about the Germans living in America, even here in Charlottesville. Which side did they want to win? Were they going to be in favor of the Nazis, or us? Otto claimed he backed the Allies, and that's about all I knew about him.

Aunt Cora said breakfast was ready, so there was no more time to think about the German stuff. She and Nat sat down, and we started eating. *Boy*, it was delicious!

While we were eating, I glanced around. Like Uncle Matthew, Dad is a pretty good woodworker. He built the wooden cabinets, even made the knobs on the doors. While we ate, I could look out through the screen door. I could see our big barn with the loft upstairs. The barn doors gaped open like a huge yawn. Behind the barn were the orchards. The lines of fruit trees went back more than the length of a football field. I liked seeing our orchards.

"Morning," I said, between bites.

"Morning," Dad and Nat said, almost in unison, and Aunt Cora smiled again. Pouring syrup on her eggs, she passed around the bottle. I glanced over at Nat, and she flicked her eyes at me like *Why don't you just eat, brother?*

I grinned. She had her hair in a ponytail. Lots of the people like ponytails, but I don't. They make a teenage girl look more like an elementary school kid. Anyway, I knew my 14-year-old sister loved school, and like me, she earned good grades. Nat loved farm life too. Both of us liked riding horses. Of course, Nat liked hanging around with her best friend, Wanda Winston. Wanda and Nat were both 9th graders this year, and had the same teachers.

My sister and I felt close, maybe because we were just thirteen months apart in age. Sure, we argued a lot, but we shared a few chores like raking the garden and caring for the horses. I never told her, but I think she's pretty neat, even though she won't help me muck out the horse stalls.

I polished off my eggs, four slices of bacon, two slices of toast with strawberry jam, and a nice, tall glass of milk. We were ready for a big day. Altogether, our family owned 100 acres. We had half an acre of various vegetables, and large fields for corn and wheat. We also had apple trees. Boy, did we have *apple trees*!

In our orchard we mostly grew Albemarle Pippins. Dad said Pippins used to be the favorite apple of Thomas Jefferson. Of course, Jefferson was the third President, following George Washington and John Adams. Anyway, we also had trees that yielded Virginia White and Red Delicious apples.

Except for during the winter, when nothing was left to harvest, we sold vegetables or fruit to neighbors and to the closest store, Jack's Grocery, usually on Saturday. We also had a whole acre of white potatoes. Believe me, that's a lot of potatoes to dig! Also, the forty acres of wheat we harvested was sent straight to the grain elevator in Charlottesville.

We kept four horses, two for plowing. After breakfast, I would feed them. At the same time, Nat would pick a basket of apples. As people like to say, "An apple a day keeps the doctor away." I hope they're right, because I eat two or three every day.

Nat and I were a few minutes into our chores when Dad called from the back door. We dropped what we were doing and raced to the house, and naturally my sister had to elbow me on the way! Dad was out on the back porch, and he grinned. "Ah, I see you're going strong on another sunny day!" I thought his face looked a little long, but I kept that to myself.

"First, though, I need you to take these bags of potatoes over to Mister Herman next door."

CHAPTER 2: Otto Herman

At our father's request, I scooped up the biggest bag of potatoes, and Nat picked up the other bag. Dad smiled. "Mister Herman can use these potatoes. I heard he's got company."

I knew Nat had done some cleaning for him a couple of times a week in the past two summers. Mister Herman usually paid her with a silver dollar, which amounted to 50 cents a day, or 25 cents per hour. The minimum wage in America is 30 cents an hour. So when Otto could pay any teenager *half* as much as he pays my sister, it made me suspicious. Why do that? Can he be *trusted* alone with her?

Dad likes Otto, so I'm kind of careful what I say about Mister Herman. Everyone knows he grew up in Germany and moved here before the war. Well, I think there's a darker side. Secretly he might support Hitler, the Nazis, and the so-called Third Reich.

"Good old Otto" is shorter than Dad, and fat, with thick arms, and likely weighs 200. Once upon a time he was probably the perfect Nordic type the Germans seem to idealize, the piercing blue eyes, the close-cropped blonde hair, and the ramrod straight posture. Now his blue eyes seem almost bulging, his blonde hair is not close-cropped, his posture is heavyset, tipping the scales at well over 200. He comes across like a big friendly Santa with a pug nose, but to me he's a little *too friendly.*

Regardless, they say Otto is a happy drinker, and that impresses lots of people. I've heard some of Dad's friends joke that Otto is a moonshiner who runs his own still out of the barn. I've also heard our father mention more than once that Otto invites the local farmers to his house for drinking parties, including, believe it or not, a couple of sheriff's deputies. So you see, it's not unusual to see a line of cars parked in his driveway on any given night.

To me it's disappointing that our father, who's an occasional drinker, will walk over to Otto's in the evening every now and then, and together they hoist a drink or two. Not only that, but my sister and I know that Dad likes to attend an occasional drinking party. Nat and I *hate drinking*, especially after the way Mom was killed.

Walking along the road with the potatoes, I wondered if I could persuade Nat to check on my suspicions, but she was rattling on about her friend Wanda Winston. Nat wanted me to know Wanda had a "crush" on some 10th grader, so I just listened and smiled.

We turned into Mister Herman's driveway. He's a widower. His wife passed away from pneumonia in early 1941. There was a big funeral in Charlottesville, and plenty of folks, including us, came and paid their respects. Nowadays Otto lives alone in the big two-story white Victorian, and like us, he owns one of those big red barns.

His house needs some repairs, but like most people we know, he owns a telephone, a refrigerator, and a radio. Telephones in our area are fairly new, but doesn't everyone have a radio? We like listening to the big band music on Station WRVA, and maybe Otto does too. His barn has that weathered look, but it's home for his two plow horses. Dad said Otto owns 100 acres too, but most of his fields are overrun with weeds.

Oddly, just as I was thinking about Otto, Nat said, "I wonder why Mister Herman never grows crops? I thought *everyone* who lives on a farm grows *something*."

I glanced at her. "Who knows? Maybe he's too old to do all the seeding, plowing, and harvesting. Or maybe he's got a *secret* business."

"Maybe," she said, "but if you ask me, growing nothing but weeds is *strange*."

Her remark made me think, *Maybe Nat has some doubts about him too*. We reached the front porch, and I glanced up at the American flag hanging on a pole sideways from the right corner of the porch. I thought *Otto sure wants people to know he's a patriot*. Nat looked up at the flag too, and rolled her eyes.

We climbed the two steps to his veranda. It was painted black and ran the width of the house. Crossing it, I knocked on the front door. The door was red with a triangular peep window trimmed with gold molding. If I remember what we learned about Germany, their flag was a black, red, and gold tricolor.

We waited, but nobody came. I knocked again, this time a little louder. "Maybe he's out in the back, or in the barn," Nat observed. "He owns a couple of horses. I've seen him riding the brown mare with the long mane a few times."

I nodded. "Yeah, that's probably it."

Carrying the bags of potatoes, which were getting heavier by the minute, we walked around the side of the house. As we passed the first window, which was raised half way, we heard two voices arguing. I recognized one as Otto's, but the other wasn't familiar. I crouched beside the house, and beckoned to Nat. She looked at me kind of funny, heard Otto roar something in a foreign language, and she ducked in front of me.

Now she looked frightened. She raised her eyebrows in a question. I held a forefinger to my lips to say *Be quiet*, and whispered, "They're speaking German."

Shuddering, she whispered, "I've *never* heard Otto speak *German*."

I raised my finger again. The two voices argued in German for a minute, getting louder and louder. Finally, the second voice declared, "*Heil, Hitler*!" At that moment I heard something click together.

Suddenly the men stopped like someone had clamped their mouths shut. We looked at each other as Otto declared, "Stop talking! You're standing close to the open window, and your voice carries. Let's go to my office."

I looked up, afraid of being seen, but the window stayed open. We heard the sound of footsteps fading away. A few seconds later, a car honked on the road out front. It occurred to me that someone was beeping *Hi!* to Otto.

Slowly I stood up. Peeking around the window edge, I looked in but couldn't see anyone. Suddenly the same idea hit us, and we looked down at the bags of potatoes which we had set down. Bending over, I grabbed my bag, and Nat, taking the cue, took hers too. I tilted my head toward the front porch. We slipped around the corner and placed the bags on the second step.

I whispered, "Let's go." We walked to the driveway, and nobody called out. It seemed to take forever to reach the road, and when we got there, I breathed a sigh of relief. I was thinking *We heard something today we weren't supposed to hear.*

At our driveway, Nat said, "Actually, there's something I need to tell you about Otto." I looked over, and her eyes were troubled. "The first time I went to work for him, two summers ago when I was twelve, he talked about my name." She looked off in the distance like people do when they're remembering.

"I told him my name is really Natalia, but my friends call me Nat." He looked at me kind of funny, and he said, 'You are called *Nat*? What is this *nat*? When I am in the weeds, an insect that buzzes around my face is a nat. You are *no* nat.'

"I said the insect is spelled g-n-a-t. I am N-a-t, short for Natalia. It's a nickname. I like it."

"Otto looked at me, and in a minute, he said, 'Then I will call you Natalia.' He said it slowly like he could taste each syllable. 'Natalia is a beautiful name, and it is perfect for you, because you are a *beautiful* young girl.' Then he gave me his huge smile, his thick cheeks crinkled, and his blue eyes kind of fluttered at me. I know, because I wrote all of it in my diary.

"Maybe he did *hook* me with his charming ways." She glanced at me. "Nobody ever called me 'beautiful,' especially my *big brother*." That sounded like a sarcastic swipe, but I let it go.

"And Otto is always a gentleman whenever I am around." She smiled, and we headed for the house. "He treats me like a princess." Suddenly her expression changed. "Maybe he is a German spy." Her greenish eyes looked bright. She was excited.

At the front door, Nat stopped and looked at me. "James, we need to talk a little more about this. You tell Dad we took the potatoes to Otto, and I'll get going with my washing and ironing."

"Okay, I'll tell him, but I'm not saying a word about what we heard."

She nodded at me, and we went into the living room. We both knew there was more to Otto than what meets the eye. I remember thinking *He's dangerous, all right. He revealed himself today.*

Nat grinned at me. "I've got some ideas too, James."

She brushed her hair back with her left hand, like she does when she's about to make a point. Grinning, she lowered her voice like a conspirator passing along a secret. "I might have recognized the other guy's voice."

"You're kidding!"

"Nope. About a week ago a friend of his family from New York City came to Otto's farm for a few weeks. He drives the blue Dodge parked at the end of the driveway, where Otto parks his black Oldsmobile. Otto introduced him to me as Derek Miller, and he seems nice enough. He's kind of good-looking with blue eyes and blond hair. He's older than us … I'd say twenty-something. He's got that peculiar strong voice you heard, kind of like he's angry. Anyway, we got acquainted, and he mentioned finishing high school three years ago."

I thought about seeing Derek and hearing his eager *Heil, Hitler!* In my mind I could see him as a Nazi fanatic. Regardless, we needed to know more about him. "What else, Nat?"

"Well, *two* can play the spy game." Nat gave me her sly grin. "In fact, maybe we could get some friends in on spying, too."

"Wait a minute, Nat! We don't want to get out of control on this thing."

She frowned. "Remember, I can easily be the 'inside' spy. Think of me as a *double agent*!" She bowed like she was making a grand gesture on stage. "I'll be there maybe three afternoons a week all summer. I'm *bound* to pick up a few secrets, especially if I don't push it."

Now she really had me thinking, and she tossed out another hook. "What have we got to lose? C'mon, James, this is *your idea*, remember?"

Suddenly I thought, *Uh-oh, she's going off half cocked.*

Like a sailor, I took another tack. I grabbed her, and hugged her, and sort of jostled her hair. Then I gave her my smoothest smile, the one I usually reserve for Dad and our teachers.

"*Oh, No*! Not the hair, James!" I had her groaning. "Oh, please, *anything* but the hair!"

She tried to fix her hair as soon as I let her go, so sure enough, I caught her off guard. I was thinking about the German voices when a practical thought hit me: I have to mow the yard today.

"C'mon, Nat. Let's get our chores done. We can worry about being teenage spies later."

CHAPTER 3: Last Week of School

It seemed like the final week of school flew by like a hound dog chasing a rabbit. Everyone was talking about plans for the summer. Several of my friends were going to play summer league baseball, and we were already signed up for the teams. I have one friend who is traveling out West to visit relatives. Harry Dixon has an Uncle Zachary who lives with his family in Boulder, Colorado, and Harry really wants to see Pikes Peak. Nat's friend Wanda says she's going with her family to Washington, DC. Wanda wants to see the Washington Monument, the Lincoln Memorial, and famous buildings like the White House. Actually nobody gets too serious in the last week of school. We get report cards on the final Friday, and I know I've got at least a "B" average. Nat might get all "A's."

Bright and early on Friday, the last day of school, my alarm clock rang like a church bell. Opening my eyes, I took a look, and there was the robin on the window ledge. He looked at me and belted out a *chirr*. I rolled out of bed, got to my feet, and stretched my arms. Geez, I was excited! Today was the last day at Jefferson High for the 1941-42 year. I kept thinking *We'll have work to do, but we'll have lots of fun too.*

I pulled on my green checked shirt, my best tan slacks, and my black school shoes. Lacing them up, I stood up and smiled. Off I went, bouncing down the stairs to breakfast. It looked like a nice morning, and Nat and I ate in a hurry. As usual, Aunt Cora was hustling around the kitchen and smiling, offering more bacon and eggs, and hovering like a mother hen. Thinking about it, she hovers a lot.

Dad had already eaten breakfast, finished the paper, and left. When I asked, Cora said, "He's gone out in the orchards. I'm not sure what he's doing on this *beautiful* morning." She sang a little "*Tra la la*" while she moved here and there. She always seems upbeat, and maybe she knows more about Dad's doings then she would say.

No matter. At 8:05 Nat and I tore out of the house and hurried along the driveway. We had to walk all the way into town in twenty minutes, giving us a couple of minutes with friends before the last day of classes started. The sun was getting warmer, the morning felt pleasant, and summer was almost here. I smiled, knowing fun times were coming. My year in the 10th grade was almost over!

About halfway to school Nat remarked, "You know, Aunt Cora has a sweet spot for Otto." She smiled at me, that mischievous smile she turns on when she knows something I don't. Stopping, I looked her in the eyes.

She was wearing bright red lipstick that she found in the vanity cabinet in the bathroom where there's still some of our mother's unused cosmetics. The lipstick, a touch of makeup, and the way she brushed her hair gave her a more grown-up look. I liked it, but kept quiet. A compliment like that coming from Walt Bunker or one of my friends might be treasured, but if her brother made it, she would feel uneasy.

Stopping, I looked Nat in the eyes. "Aunt Cora and *Otto*? Wait a minute! What makes you think *that*?"

"Well, you know, she's been walking over there with a bag of apples once or twice a week. Once I saw her taking a bag with tomatoes, and two or three times she was taking green beans." She grinned at me like I didn't get it.

"Maybe you didn't notice, James, but remember last week when she fixed cornbread? She baked *four* loaves. Well, we ate *one*, and she put *two* in the refrigerator."

She flicked her sly smile. "The last loaf *somehow* found its way into a bag with a few Albemarle Pippins. When I saw her touching up her hair and getting ready to leave with the bag, I played it *very casually*. I said, 'Gee, are we going to have enough cornbread?'

"Aunt Cora is bright, and she anticipated me. She gives me one of her *sweet smiles*, and she says, 'Cornbread doesn't keep real well in the fridge. So … I thought Mister Herman might like *fresh* cornbread. He's not much of a cook, you know. Your father says he eats mostly canned food from the grocery store.'"

Nat turned on the big grin. "She used Dad to try to slip that one past me, so I tried a little flattery. I said, 'Gee, Aunt Cora. That's *very thoughtful* of you.' And before she could give me some clever answer, I said, 'Do you want *me* to carry the cornbread to Mister Herman?'

"I surprised her for a moment, and she gave me a funny look. But quick as a wink, she flashed a gushy smile. 'Don't worry,' she said. 'I'll have some extra time after I do the dishes. I want to take a walk anyway …'"

"What do you think of that, *Mister Spy*?"

I gave her a skeptical look. "C'mon, Nat. You're still talking about teenage spying. But all we heard was a conversation in German topped off by the words Heil Hitler. For all we know, Otto and his friend might have been talking about the evils of Nazism, and when the other guy said Heil Hitler, maybe he was mocking Nazism. What about that, huh?"

Nat glanced at me, didn't reply, and I knew what I said gave her food for thought. As it turned out, we made it to school with a minute or two to spare. By the time the 8:30 bell rang, I was sitting in Mister Bronston's Social Studies class. I looked around at the familiar room. The dull blue walls looked like they needed a fresh coat of paint. His old wooden desk occupied a place of honor on the left side. The blackboard took up most of the front wall. Above it, the American flag was hanging from a pole attached to the wall next to the door with its window to the hallway. As usual, Bronston was standing behind his desk at the blackboard and holding a piece of chalk. He likes to stand there, toss the chalk up, and catch it like a signal to pay attention. This morning he gave the class his stern look.

"Stand for the Pledge," he said, in his usual monotone, coming to attention himself. We all stood up in the rows on the left side of the desks. Like the others, I placed my right arm over my heart, and together the class recited the familiar words: "I pledge allegiance to the flag of the United States of America …" Saying those words usually brought tears to my eyes, but I wasn't alone. "… and to the Republic for which it stands, one nation indivisible, with liberty and justice for all."

"*Be seated*," he declared, and we resumed our wooden desks. I heard one or two whispered words behind me, but whoever it was shut up quickly. *No point in stirring up the teacher this last week*, I thought. Skipping the roll call, Bronston drew a large outline of the United States in the middle of the blackboard. Nodding at it, he outlined the Pacific Ocean. After that, he drew some tiny circles for the

Hawaiian Islands. He looked at us, turned, and marked Pearl Harbor with an X. Nodding at his handiwork, he did his chalk-tossing number a few times.

Bronston had all of us listening, and his voice rose a notch as he pointed to the X. He had a personal interest in the events at Pearl Harbor, and most of us had heard about it. Frowning, he chalked the names of a few Navy ships on the blackboard. Of course, the chalk would *squeak*, making some of us shudder. I think he did it for emphasis. Tossing the chalk again, he looked at us.

By mid-1941 the Navy, he declared solemnly, had stationed nearly 100 warships at Pearl Harbor. Stopping, he tossed the chalk. The ship that had suffered the most damage was the battleship *Arizona*. The newspapers, he emphasized, reported more than 2,000 Americans, mostly sailors and soldiers, were killed in the Japanese bombing of December 7, 1941. Eying us, Bronston quietly quoted FDR, calling it "a date that will live in infamy."

Hearing about Pearl Harbor again made me angry. Tears came to my eyes, but like the rest of the class, I kept quiet. It was a reverential moment, almost like hearing prayer at church.

Of course, Bronston wasn't done. Next he talked about Albert, his older brother, and his voice got quiet. Albert was a gunner's mate on the *Arizona*. He's still listed as "Missing in Action," but the way Bronston talks about it, you can tell he expects the worst.

All we could do was listen. I guess most everyone's family has some relatives who served on an American ship in the Pacific. When the Japanese bombed us, on *Sunday* morning no less, they sure caught everyone off guard. They're clever, all right, and I guess we didn't have much of a chance. Sooner or later the US will pay them back for that sneak attack, and I sure hope they *pay big.*

While those thoughts were running through my mind, the bell rang. I grabbed my books and hurried off to Math class. Boy, the whole atmosphere was different! Miss Whitmore was making us do long division, *again.* She passed out a page of problems, and we had to take turns doing one on the blackboard. But when I went back to my seat, my thoughts wandered back to Otto and Derek being Nazi spies.

Later, in study hall, I was whispering whenever the teacher, Coach Duncan, also our football coach, looked somewhere else. Mainly I was talking to Walt Bunker, who sits behind me. Walt doesn't live far away, and we're going to play summer ball. We play on the same team, so we can get together and pitch batting practice to each other.

When the lunch bell rang, I jumped up and headed for the cafeteria. My stomach was already telling me it was time to eat! When I walked in the double doors, I spotted Adam Zimmerman at a corner table. The cafeteria is a long, high-ceilinged room painted light orange. On the wall facing the playground there's a row of tall windows. The inside wall has a large mural of Monticello painted by the local WPA Project. I heard our principal, Mister Adams, painted most of the mural, but nobody knows for sure. The counter with the trays and dishes and tableware and food is on the back wall, in front of the kitchen. I headed for Adam's table.

At the same time Nat came through the big arched doorway, and she saw me and Adam. My sister made it to the corner table about the same time I did. When we sat down, the teasing started.

"Really, James," said Paul Falkner, another 10th grader. "You're bringing your 'girlfriend' to sit with us?" Several guys at the next table heard it, and they all began laughing and joking.

"What? C'mon, Paul! Get over it. You know she's my sister!"

A couple of 11th graders joined in the teasing, but Nat and I stood up and left for the food counter. We had to wait behind a bunch of seniors. They were laughing and horsing around, because they were done for good. Anyway, who's serious on the last day of school? We pushed our trays through the line and picked up lunch. The day's menu was one Sloppy Joe, a scoop of corn, and a Pippin apple. I guess it was Jefferson High's budget farewell to the year!

Back at the table, both of us sat down and started eating. After a bite of my Sloppy Joe, I leaned close to Adam. "Your Uncle Rolf grew up in Germany, right?"

"Look," Adam whispered. "I'm a patriot."

Of course, I knew having a German family member bothered Adam. As most of us knew, people didn't want to be associated with anything German while the United States was fighting a war with Nazi Germany and fascist Italy.

I glanced at Adam. "Relax, buddy. I know you're an American. But here's what I'm wondering. If you overheard a couple of guys speaking German these days, what would you think?"

Eying me, he frowned. "Look, James. Every now and then I get grief about our German 'background,' and I hate it. My Mom and Dad hate it too, and Uncle Rolf, he *really* hates it."

"I understand, Adam." I glanced at him. "So, does your Uncle Rolf have friends that speak German when they get together?"

Adam looked at me like I had a hole in my head. "You're kidding me, right?"

When I shook my head no, he whispered, "No, they don't. I heard Dad say a few days ago that anything *German* is taboo. It turns out Uncle Rolf asked him not to speak German *anywhere*. He's pretty nervous."

I was surprised by Adam's response, and I never even mentioned the *Heil, Hitler*. Thinking quickly, I shifted gears.

"Relax. I won't say anything, except maybe to my sister. But Nat won't say anything either." Looking around, I whispered, "Except maybe to her girlfriend, Wanda."

Adam gave me his goofy grin. "I know Wanda. She's kind of nice, so yeah, that's okay."

By coincidence, Wanda spotted us at the corner table. In no time she arrived with her tray and sat next to Nat. They shared "girl stuff" while Adam and I talked about baseball in the town's Summer B League for guys ages no more than high school age. A little after 12:45, the four of us got up, took our trays with the dirty dishes back to the counter, and headed for the 1:00 classes.

The afternoon seemed to drag along, but finally the last bell rang at 3:00. By then everyone had turned in their school books. We trooped down the hall and out on the sidewalk in front. Everyone spent time talking to schoolmates and saying goodbyes to friends. I spoke to a few guys who will play in the summer league. Smiling, I realized next spring I would be playing varsity baseball for the school, and maybe start at first base or left field. I couldn't wait. The varsity plays two games a week for six weeks, and the JVs just play once a week. When I get to be 18, maybe the coach will pick me for the town ball team, just like my Dad before me.

Walking home with Nat, I told her how Adam said his uncle and his parents were not going to speak any German anywhere. He didn't even want me to repeat what he said for fear of stirring up feelings against his family. I stopped and looked my sister in the eye. "So, what do you think about that?"

Nat sighed, and shook her head. "It tells me what we heard was a bigger deal than we thought." She studied me for a moment. "Did you tell Adam about the 'Heil, Hitler' quote?"

"Nope," I replied, starting to walk again. "I did not."

She hurried to catch up. "Well, James. I'd say it's time to do some teenage spying!"

CHAPTER 4: New Neighbors

After making it home on Friday afternoon, Nat and I changed clothes, went out to the barn, and started grooming the horses. I kept quiet at first, and finally she got tired of waiting. "Why don't *we* become spies?"

I played it carefully. "That could be dangerous, you know. What exactly do you have in mind?"

"We can spy on Otto ourselves, like I said when we walked back from Otto's place the other day. This summer I'll be working at his house, and when he's outside, I can poke around and maybe find things. I know he's got an 'office,' as he calls it, where I'm not supposed to clean. I guess he keeps his papers and bills and letters there where he can lay his hands on them. On my very first day of cleaning, he showed me around the house, but he said to leave his office alone. 'It's just my desk,' he said, 'a couple of chairs, and an old file cabinet with my records.'"

She brushed back her brown hair, but a few strands fell over one greenish eye. "In fact, I haven't even been in his office. He always keeps the door shut and locked. I know, because I tried it once when he was on the front porch. The office is on the back side of the house, so he can look out and see his yard and the barn. He's got a radio in there, because sometimes I hear him playing music or listening to the news with the door closed."

I listened carefully as my sister talked about the office. She was eager to move ahead with spying, and it scared me a little. I thought about cautioning her, but would she listen? Not likely. The ball was rolling now, and I thought we might learn something important.

"Maybe it can't be *too* dangerous." I grinned. "After all, we're in Charlottesville, not New York City."

Even as the thought came to mind, I realized that I was the older one, and I would be held responsible if something went wrong. As soon as I thought about it, I knew Dad would see it that way. Again I looked at her. "I don't think Dad would like this, not one little bit."

"We aren't going to tell him, right?" She turned those bright eyes on me like twin x-rays. "You know, if something dangerous does come up, we can tell Dad. But we don't know if I'll find anything important, right?"

"No, but here's the deal. Any time you're at Otto's house and do anything besides routine stuff, like looking around his office, you write it in your diary when you come home. Afterward, you show me, and I do mean *not* very long afterward, Nat."

I gave her a frown, and she let out a long sigh. "Oh, *all right*." She started with her pouty voice, the one she uses when she doesn't get her way, but in a flash she dropped it. "I guess it might be *safer* to write everything down. Yes, and I'll also tell you too. But we can't have Dad or Aunt Cora nearby where they can hear it."

I felt relieved when she agreed, and we shook hands on it. We went back to grooming the horses. Once we finished, I pulled the old lawn mower out of the shed beside the barn. I checked the blades, and they were sharp. I pushed the mower faster than usual, first cutting the lawn in front all the way to the road, and then doing the back yard from the house to the barn. Altogether, that chore took me well over an hour. The sun was beginning to slip down in the western sky when I put the mower away.

Heading to our back yard well, I took a few swigs of cool water with the metal dipper that hangs under the little square roof. Boy, I needed that water! No sooner had I replaced the dipper when Aunt Cora stepped out onto the back porch and waved. I knew what she wanted. She prepares dinner practically on the dot of 6:00.

"C'mon, James! Your Dad and Nat are getting cleaned up."

She flashed that sweet smile. I smiled back, and again I realized Cora felt like we were like her children. I didn't mind, though, because she was always so nice. If we did anything wrong, she just told Dad. No doubt she shied away from any discipline because she knew we'd fault her. I smiled. Our aunt was clever.

That Friday evening we had roast beef, green beans, mashed potatoes, fried squash, and tall glasses of water; Dad and Aunt Cora also had cups of coffee. They like coffee at every meal. While we were eating, Nat regaled us about the last day of school. To hear her tell it, you'd think she and Wanda were the two most popular girls in the 9th grade. A couple of boys were talking to them after school ended, and they just knew they were about to be asked on a movie date.

The movie date never materialized, but the only thing we didn't hear about it was the names of the boys. She said one of them spoke about seeing *The Maltese Falcon*, which is showing at the Paramount on Main Street. That's a mile from our house. A couple of friends and I saw that movie one Saturday last summer, so they must be bringing it back. Humphrey Bogart is the big star, and Peter Lorre, the famous British actor, and Mary Astor, the pretty brunette, also starred in that film.

"Bogey," as they call him, doesn't look to me like a big hero, but he impresses plenty of fans. Earlier this week in the cafeteria I heard a couple of seniors talking about *Maltese Falcon*. Of course, I knew Bogart played a private eye in San Francisco, and I like seeing places like that where movies are actually filmed. I probably won't ever see San Francisco outside the theater. But maybe when I grow up, go to college, and do some traveling, I can go out West.

After Nat raved about the movie, I told Dad and Aunt Cora about playing baseball in the summer league. I know plenty of friends who will play too. Dad has met some of them like Jack Jones, Walt Bunker, and Herb Jenkowski. All four of us played for the Broncos last summer, and maybe we'll have a better team this year.

While we were polishing off the apple pie, Dad told us what he read about America's war effort in the Pacific Ocean soon after it happened in the second week of May. He calmly observed that not too long ago, the Navy had handed the Japanese a major defeat in Japan's part of the Pacific.

He mentioned something else I remember we heard in class. Mister Bronston said it was the first time in history that America had won a naval battle when neither side actually saw the other side's ships. In other words, the fighter planes on both sides kept on dog-fighting each other. At the movies one Saturday, they showed the same kind of airplane fighting over England in the Movietone

News. It's simple. I think the Americans and the English have the best pilots.

Anyway, after Dad talked about the Coral Sea, Aunt Cora chimed in and said Otto had a family friend, Derek Miller, visiting from New York City for the summer. Right away she got my attention, because this was the voice Nat said we heard saluting Hitler under Otto's window.

"According to Otto," Aunt Cora said, "Derek graduated from high school a few years ago. I guess Otto needs help on his farm this summer." She smiled sweetly. "He told me he would like to clear some land behind his barn, and maybe start farming it."

Aunt Cora knew more about Otto than I realized. Suddenly it dawned on me that she must have had quite a conversation with Otto himself, because how else would she know? When the thought hit me, Nat and I exchanged a knowing look. Actually, it felt like we were on the same wave length. Giving me a quick smile, she looked to Aunt Cora, who was rambling on about how Otto didn't have enough fresh food. "I'm going to take him a bag of Pippins tomorrow."

That got me thinking. Is Aunt Cora "sweet" on Otto, just like Nat said? If she likes him, she might repeat some tidbits that could help Nat and I figure out what Otto is involved with at home, especially in his office.

A week earlier at dinner on Friday evening, Dad had been talking about William Martin, an older neighbor of ours who lost his wife to pneumonia two years ago. He told us Mister Martin is engaged to his "pen pal" from

Raleigh, North Carolina. Dad smiled about it, and he told us he planned to build a bed and dresser set for him. He said it was nice to give someone a good gift when they were planning to marry.

Tonight after dessert, Dad and Aunt Cora went out to sit on the porch and enjoy the rest of the evening, and I followed Nat up to her bedroom. She handed me a medium-sized book bound in blue leather with the words *My Diary* printed in gold on the front. She opened it to a certain page, and showed me where to start reading.

She grinned. "This is part of our agreement for me to find out more about Otto."

I looked at her, and she smiled. This is what I read: "Two days ago I met Karl Ellis, who just finished the 11th grade in high school in New York City. He's a nephew of Otto Herman and the son of Otto's sister Elsa, who died a few years after he was born. Karl's father Lionel Ellis, a chemist, teaches Chemistry at New York University. Karl plans to go to the same university when he finishes high school, but he wants to do something different for the summer. His uncle talked with his father, and they agreed farm work for a couple of months would benefit him.

"He said he met his Uncle Otto a couple of times when he was visiting them in New York City. The day I met Karl at Otto's house, he looked at me kind of special. I can tell he likes me. After I finished the cleaning, he asked me to go for a walk around the two farms. I think Otto embarrassed him when we were getting ready for the walk.

"Otto smiled at me, and said, 'Remember, Karl is a city boy, and he doesn't know a cow pie from a mud pie!' Otto laughed like he cracked the funniest joke in the world, but Karl's cheeks were burning, so I knew he was really embarrassed.

"Maybe to make up for it, Otto suggested to Karl that we walk to our farm, and he called the Bakers his friends as well as his neighbors. He told Karl that our father is an 'honorable man' who allows his daughter to help a 'poor widower' keep his house clean. Again he laughed, but not as much this time. All this makes me think Otto likes to look happy and carefree, but who really knows?

"Otto said I should introduce Karl to my brother. But instead, we walked all the way to the back of Otto's land and over to the wooden bench under the large oak tree behind our orchards. We sat there for a while and talked. He put his arm around me, and we snuggled. Everything was nice. By the time we came back, I needed to get home for dinner. Anyway, Karl is really nice, so I'll introduce him to Dad and James."

When I finished reading, I looked at Nat. Flashing her quick smile, she blushed. I asked, "What do you think of Karl? He's not much older than us. I'm surprised Otto wanted his nephew to come and stay two months when he's already got Derek Miller staying with him."

"I don't know, James. But I like him, and I can tell he likes *me*. No other boy at our school ever *liked* me before, so that's nice. He even kissed me once, and I was sure surprised!"

For a few moments her cheeks turned as red as a fire truck. Looking at me, she added, "I don't think Karl believes in the stuff we heard Otto and Derek arguing about. Really, I guess I'll have to get to know him better, and find out."

I saw the blush on her cheeks and the twinkle in her eyes. "Neither one of us has a mother, you know. So far, so good!"

Nodding at her, I heard myself agreeing. And I thought *Maybe this crazy teen spy idea might be worthwhile after all. But first we need to find out more about Derek Miller and Karl Ellis.*

CHAPTER 5: Baseball Practice

On Saturday morning after breakfast I was walking to the barn, and Nat called out. Turning, I saw her standing near the back porch with a guy I didn't know. "James, I want you to meet my friend Karl."

I did a double take as they headed toward me. She was wearing a goofy grin and holding his hand, but he seemed reluctant, like maybe he was afraid of me. When they got close, he gave me an awkward smile. I figured my best bet was to be friendly. "You must be Karl." I grinned. "Nat has told me a little about you."

We shook hands like old friends. At a glance, Karl looked about six feet tall. He had blue eyes, a thin nose, and dark wavy hair. "It's nice to meet you, James. Your sister tells me you plan to be a writer when you finish high school." He smiled again. "I hope that works out for you."

Offering my smile, I rolled my eyes. "Nat might have jumped the gun, Karl. Yes, I would like to write historical fiction, but first, I plan to attend the University of Virginia, here in Charlottesville. I understand their Literature Department is tops in the state, and I'll need to learn a *lot*. Maybe someday I'll be smart enough to be a good writer."

Karl's face flushed. "Well, I didn't mean to presume … Uh, I meant your sister really does speak rather highly of you."

With that comment we all smiled. "I understand, but relax. I'm happy to meet you, and I hope you enjoy your time on your Uncle Otto's farm. He's rather well liked locally." Grinning, I glanced at Nat. "Wouldn't you say so, Sis?"

She took my cue. "Yes, we understand your uncle is well thought of in the community. I like the cleaning and stuff he pays me to do, but, of course, it's *hardly* exciting." She smiled at Karl. "Still, he's always pleasant."

Eying me, Nat shifted gears. "Karl's mother died not long after he was born. None of us have a mother, so we all have that in common." Again she smiled at Karl, and this time his face reddened.

He looked at me as if for support. "Yes, my father, Lionel Ellis, has always been there for me. He comes to the school whenever he needs to see my teachers. He came to the junior play, 'You Can't Take It with You,' when I was Boris, a Russian dance instructor. Father found me a part-time job in Dierdorf's Grocery, on the corner of our street. I'm pretty fortunate, even if my mother did die. And Uncle Otto," and his eyes sparkled. "Well, he's our closest relative here in America."

I listened to his story. Karl seemed like other teenagers, because most of us have faced something going wrong in our family. Before I could reply, Nat cut in. "Karl and I are going to take a walk before I do my chores. But I wanted you two to meet." She gave me a quick smile. "Tell Dad I'll be back after a while."

Smiling at Karl, she took his hand, and they headed along the driveway. As I watched them walk away, I could guess why she liked him. Karl was a year or two older than me, sounded earnest, and looked handsome. He reminded me of young Joseph Cotton, the famous actor. I smiled to myself, knowing sooner or later Nat would work Karl for information.

Still, Nat's eyes gave away her feelings, and another thought hit me. Making a mental note to listen carefully to what she reported, I figured she was falling for the guy. And of course, her being in love wasn't part of the plan. Sighing, I headed for the barn.

An hour later, when my chores were finished, I came back inside and went up to my bedroom to change. In the dresser I found my blue shirt with B-r-o-n-c-o-s in orange letters across the front. Pulling it on, I found it a bit tight. From the closet I grabbed my dark blue baseball cap, my Spalding glove, and my worn baseball spikes. I checked myself in the mirror, and the shirt looked okay. Satisfied, I packed the gear in my gym bag. I found Dad out in back and told him where I was going. Looking at me, he grinned, and I took off walking toward the baseball field behind our high school.

Along the road I ran into Walt Bunker, our shortstop, who lives three farms closer to town. We walked along side-by-side, and mostly we talked about last summer's team. The Broncos took third place in the Boys B League. Of course, we hoped to have a better team this summer. Walt, who's about my size with brown eyes and hair, and a quick sense of humor, looked excited. Both of us were looking forward to the first practice.

As we reached town, Walt cracked, "Maybe the Broncos will turn into horses this year!"

A few minutes before 10:00 we arrived at the diamond behind the school. Coach Spencer, our baseball and basketball coach, arrived ahead of us, and so did a few of our buddies. Besides Walt, my closest friends on the team were Jack Jones, who plays the outfield, and Herb Jenkoski, our catcher. The coach had everyone warming up, playing catch with each other. We knew the routine. After the warm-ups he'd set us down for a pep talk about the practice for that day. Afterward, the coach would hit some ground balls to the infield, and the assistant would knock fly balls to the outfielders. Stashing my bag under the bottom row of the bleachers, I laced on my spikes and adjusted my cap. I liked wearing it with the brim pulled low.

Standing up, I looked around at the familiar surroundings. The school had a pretty good diamond. The infield was all dirt, and Ray Riley, the longtime janitor, always kept the grass mowed in the outfield. The school owned an old John Deere that Riley used to pull the well-worn drag to smooth the infield dirt. One set of bleachers flanked the third base side, and the fifteen-foot high wire backstop connected it to the other bleachers on the first base side. A six-foot chain link fence surrounded the entire field with gates at each end of the backstop and gates at each end of the bleachers.

The school had hand-painted signs posted on the foul poles in left and right field showing the distance from home plate, 285 feet in left and 275 feet in right. The back corner of the center field fence had to be more than 300 feet. There were light poles at each end of the backstop, behind first and third bases, and in each corner of the outfield. Everyone knew the big league ballparks had longer distances and better lights for night games, but the major leagues were tops in every way.

Next to the fenced-in baseball field was the football field, and it was surrounded by a chain link fence with gates for certain entry points too. Between the 40-yard lines on each side of the gridiron there was a long wooden bench for the players. A set of bleachers flanked each side of the field, but the bleachers on the home team's side were twice as long as on the visitors' side. Everything was painted blue and trimmed in orange, the school colors. Thinking about our football field, I'd say Jefferson could seat more than 2,000 at a home game.

Behind the home team's bleachers there's a wooden press box built on a 12-foot tower. The box has a roof, wooden covers for the windows, and inside there's a microphone with wires strung all the way to the speakers on the light poles. The announcer, usually Mister Gingery, our Algebra and Geometry teacher, would speak over the microphone telling the audience what happened on each play.

Ol' Gingery has been calling football games for as long as I can remember. A short balding man with wire rim glasses and a droll voice, he really knows his stuff. But he would be helped by a spotter from each team, and most of the spotters were teachers too. Each school would provide a mimeographed list of the players' names along with their numbers, positions, and height with weights. The spotter, using his list, told the announcer quietly the names of the ball carrier and the tackler, or the tacklers, and Ol' Gingery droned it into the microphone. You could hear that familiar voice beyond the gridiron on a Friday night, even over on the next street.

I think it's neat to see a football game under the lights. We play a few night games on the baseball field, but those lights aren't as bright. When you realize the infield has two light poles on each side but only three light poles surrounding the entire outfield, you can see why it's tough to judge fly balls at night games. But in the summer league, we play mostly day games. The good news is the sun doesn't set until after 8:30 in June and July, so the bright lights aren't needed as much in baseball as they are in football.

While I was thinking about the school's ball fields, Coach Spencer called us to the third base bleachers. Everyone trotted to the stands, clambered up the boards in our spikes, and sat next to a buddy. I sat beside Walt. Jack and Herb and Adam Zimmerman sat in the row behind us. There must have been a dozen of us that came to practice. Adam is annoying. He kept whispering to Herb about going to the movies, but after a couple of minutes, one evil-eye look from the coach and they clammed up.

"All right, fellas," Spencer said. "We're going out there and taking batting practice. Everyone not hitting can take the position they want to play this summer, and I'll call you up, two at a time. Herb, you put on the catcher's gear and catch first."

The coach grinned; we all knew he loves baseball. "I'll chuck 'em in there. Of course, Mister Riley will get the balls that you field and toss them back to the pitcher's box."

That wasn't a surprise. Ray Riley was the biggest baseball fan in Charlottesville. He was also a friend to most of the kids in the high school. I heard him and his wife Janet drive up to Washington to see the Senators play more than a dozen times each season. Not only that, Riley never misses a game in any sport at our high school.

Spencer nodded at Jackson next to him. "Coach Jackson will work with the outfielders, hitting fly balls while we're taking batting practice."

Mister Jackson is our gym teacher, and everyone has to take gym classes. Jackson likes to assist Spencer with baseball and football. I heard they're good friends, and their wives know each other well too. Jackson's a wiry guy about five-ten with a long face and a loud voice, and he knows a lot about every sport.

Coach Spencer waved at the diamond, and we all climbed down from the bleachers and trotted out on the field with our gloves. When the coach yelled for Bunker and Jones to bat, I moved out to left field. By then half a dozen guys were scattered around the outfield. Looking at us, Spencer started lobbing in the pitches, and sure enough, Walt cracked out three or four good shots. After about five minutes, Spencer called in another guy to warm up, Walt went to his position at shortstop, and Jack stepped up to the plate. I was sixth to hit. Altogether, we spent at least an hour in batting practice. The big surprise came when Adam took a really good cut and drove a long fly over the fence in left field. I don't remember him even hitting a double, let alone a homer. Boy, did that hit put a smile on Coach Spencer's face!

Of course, Walt, who likes ribbing other guys, couldn't resist it. When Adam was all smiles and heading for the outfield, Walt hollered, "How did we get Joe DiMaggio on our team? Next thing we know, somebody's gonna turn into Mickey Vernon or Ted Williams!"

Guys were kidding each other, and the whole practice was lighthearted. Still, that's the way summer baseball goes. If the Broncos finish higher than third in the six-team league, it won't be that big of a deal. It's not like you win a varsity letter for summer ball. Actually, everyone *likes* playing baseball, period. And if you can impress Coach Spencer, that makes it even more worthwhile. Some of us will be playing for the varsity next year, and this will be good experience.

Following the practice, Spencer handed everyone a bottle of Coca-Cola that his wife Adell brought about halfway through the session. I saw her arrive with the red metal cooler holding more than a dozen bottles in a bed of ice. The cool Coke hit the spot!

Missus Spencer always comes to the practices and the games coached by her husband. A short brunette with a peppy personality, she works part-time at the dime store downtown. She's a big fan of all Jefferson High events, and everyone likes her.

As we were sipping the soda, Adell started telling us about a dime store customer who kept buying a red potted geranium and, maybe a week later, returning the wilted geranium for a new one, claiming the original plant had died. She would come in the store, hand over the plant at the cash register, and politely insist on a new one. This lasted for about three months. Each time Adell would tell the woman, who seemed a little demented, that you had to water the geranium.

By then the other guys had departed, one by one, but Walt and I hung around mainly out of deference to the coach and his wife. At some point during practice I noticed Otto Herman and a young stranger sitting in the bleachers watching us. He was blonde, curly-haired, blue-eyed, and about six feet tall. Looking at them again, I figured it was Derek Miller. At first I was surprised when I saw them in the bleachers with what appeared to be bottles of beer, because it was just a practice. On the other hand, Otto had attended two or three Broncos games last summer. He did like attending community events like ball games, school plays, city parades, and of course, festivals.

When Adell finally finished the dime store tale, I noticed Coach Spencer off on one side shaking hands with Derek. Otto had introduced them, and the three of them were talking and smiling.

CHAPTER 6: Baseball, Otto, and Girls

When Walt and I picked up our duffel bags to leave, the three men approached us. Coach Spencer said, "Derek, meet James and Walt. Boys, Otto's friend Derek Miller here tells me he used to pitch for Albany of the Eastern League, back in 1938 and 1939. That's professional baseball, and the best players could go on to Double-A Indianapolis, and maybe even Cincinnati, in the National League. Derek said he was expected to make the big leagues, but he broke his leg after the 1939 season, and it never healed right."

The coach paused, and Derek, smiling, said, "I was crossing Fifth Avenue when a black Chauffeur-driven Cadillac ran into me, knocked me down, and sent me to the hospital. The owner, a rich woman from Long Island, hired a Jew lawyer. Well, he claimed negligence on my part, the case went to court, and I never saw a dime."

Nodding at Otto, Derek continued: "I had a stint in the Army a year later, training in demolitions. But the leg got worse with all the workouts and running, and they mustered me out."

Spencer looked annoyed. "Anyway, what I was *going* to say is Derek says that *if* you're willing, he's healed enough to pitch, and he'd be glad to throw some to you two fellas." He smiled. "It might be interesting to test your batting against someone who was once a pro pitcher headed to the major leagues."

"I can still throw as hard," Derek claimed, grinning with his eyes glowing. "But I can't hardly run at all!"

I started to reply, but Walt jumped in and said, "Sure, why not? We've got a few minutes before we need to head for home and our chores."

At that point Otto took over like the whole thing was his idea. "Walt can go to the outfield, James, just in case you actually hit one. But I warn you. Derek can throw really hard!" He was all smiles. "I can do the catching. I've caught a few games in my day."

He laughed, and the coach and Adell smiled. Evidently Otto had convinced them that two of his best summer league players ought to try to hit against a hard-throwing pitcher, a guy four or five years older with professional experience. Actually, the whole thing kind of ticked me off. But I knew if I said so, I'd look bad in the coach's eyes.

So I nodded, and Spencer looked pleased. He turned to his equipment bag, retrieved a glove and a couple of worn baseballs for Derek, and a catcher's mitt for Otto. Inside a minute Walt reached the outfield, Derek stood on the pitcher's box, and Otto squatted behind me, pounding the mitt. A right-hander, Derek wound up without much left leg kick, and he threw a few warm-up fastballs to Otto. Those pitches really smacked into the mitt. Watching them, I realized Derek was throwing harder than any high school pitcher I'd ever seen. For a few moments I felt sick.

To overcome the feeling, I took a couple of deep breaths, exhaling slowly. I had to face the challenge, or the guys would laugh at me for backing out. Being a right-handed batter, I stepped up to the left side of the plate. Moving a little dirt with my cleats so I could stand in more comfortably, I took my favorite stance, my bat cocked and held low over my right shoulder.

Knowing the coach and his wife were sitting forty feet away in the bleachers, Otto started taunting me in a low voice. Nobody but me could hear him, and at first he confused me.

"The other day, James, I looked out my window and saw you and your sister hurrying out the driveway. I got to thinking maybe you two were *spying* on me."

My face turned red, but I watched Derek throw his last warm-up. *Smack*, the mitt seemed to wince as Otto handled the pitch. Looking out of the corner of my right eye, I saw him go down on one knee and toss the ball back to Derek as easily as if he was playing baseball regularly.

"Yes, James," Otto added casually, "I found the bags of potatoes. You two *were* spying on me. You're nothing but a weakling American who turns to spying on his neighbors. You can't stand it that I didn't grow up in Virginia, like you, in a rich family. I'll bet you and your sister, and of course, your father and your mother are Jewish, right?"

He laughed quietly. "You don't want loyal citizens like Derek and myself to know your true colors. You can't stand it that we weren't *born* in the United States, the home of the free, the rich, and the Jew; in America where fools keep electing a crippled weakling for a leader."

Tears filled my eyes as he insulted me, and the whole country. I couldn't bring myself to reply, not at first. I didn't dare look at him, or he'd see the tears. Raising his voice, he called out, "Let's go, Derek! James is as ready as he'll ever be!"

Whoosh, the pitch flew by me and hit Otto's mitt with a loud *smack*. Derek, his eyes drilling into me, caught me thinking about what Otto said, and I kicked myself mentally. Getting in my stance, I shifted my feet a little, bent my knees slightly, and focused on the pitcher.

Whoosh, the next pitch flew by as I swung hard, but way late. I was embarrassed. Derek must have been telling the truth. I had never batted against any pitcher who put such speed on a baseball. All the time Otto was speaking in an undertone, taunting me, and calling me and my sister not only weak but stupid.

I dug in and got ready for another pitch. From behind me the insults continued: "Your father acts like he's a big deal, but Zeke Baker is just another sniveling fraud like all of his neighbors. All but me, buddy boy, *all but me*."

Whoosh, the pitch whizzed by, and again I swung hard and missed like I had a hole in my bat. I felt *humiliated*. I wondered, *How would I live this down*? Stepping back, I glanced over at the bleachers. Coach Spencer and Adell were looking at each other with surprised expressions.

"C'mon, James!" Walt yelled from the outfield. "Blast one for me, pal!" I could see him pounding his glove. "This guy *can't* be that good!"

Swoosh. Thunk. I missed, but this time not by as much. I held up my left hand to pause, and I moved back a step. I used my bat to knock at the dirt on my spikes, first the left shoe and then the right one. Moving back into the box, I tapped the plate with my bat, just like the pros do.

All the while I was trying to ignore Otto's insults and paying more attention to Derek's windup, his release, and where the pitch crossed the plate.

Looking in at us, Derek smiled. He went into his short windup, and he fired another fast one, this one an inside duster, and the ball whacked my left hand on the knuckles. They burned like fire, and I grunted. I took my left hand off the bat, flexed the fingers, and gripped the bat again. Looking at Derek, I realized he'd hit me on purpose.

Otto chuckled. "Well, James, it looks like Derek might be a little wild today, eh? Better watch out. He might kill you with one of his fast ones!"

He tossed the ball back. Derek snagged it, waited a few seconds, and sneered at me. Suddenly it hit me: The whole purpose of this little exhibition was for Otto and Derek to humiliate me in front of the coach and his wife and my friend. I took a deep breath while Otto chuckled like an evil magician who had penetrated my mind. I was making his day by swinging and missing at his friend's fastballs.

Again I took my stance, and without a pause, Derek took his windup and whizzed one over the outside of the plate, and swinging hard again, I managed to tick the ball, deflecting it off the bottom of Otto's mitt. *Ugghhh*, he moaned, and I looked down in time to see the ball fall to the ground in front of him. The ball must have hit his sizable gut. Sucking air, he muttered something in German.

"What's the matter, *Mister Herman*?" I could see in his eyes that he knew I wasn't giving up. "Maybe you're not as good a catcher as you *pretend*? Is that it?"

Glaring at me, he swore softly and extended the mitt. Derek winged another bullet right at me, but I saw it coming and turned away. The ball *plopped* into my left arm, and I flipped the bat to my right, sending it flying at Otto's head. Reacting, he fell backward, and I heard a *thump* as he landed on his sizable butt. Walt yelled, "Hang in there, Mister Herman!"

Straightening up, I walked toward the bat, pretending my arm didn't burn and ignoring Otto as he got slowly to one knee. "You okay, Otto?" came the worried query from Derek standing sixty feet away.

As I picked up the bat, I noticed the coach and his wife standing up with curious expressions on their faces. I knew they wondered if I flung the bat at him on purpose. Smiling to myself, I returned to the batter's box. Looking around, Walt caught my eye. He was pounding his fist into the pocket of his glove and grinning like a circus clown.

From beside me came a guttural voice: "*Mein Gott*! You almost killed me!"

"Geez, I'm sorry, Otto." It was the first time I hadn't addressed him as *Mister Herman*. "The ball was gonna hit me, and I was trying to duck out of the way. Isn't that what you'd expect a smart ballplayer to do?"

I grinned at him, knowing this was really a contest between me and Otto, not so much between me and Derek. He was really just a blonde German thug sucking up to his superior. Looking at our neighbor, my calling him *Otto* told him in a word that I was a young man ready to engage him and his lackey. In fact, I was no longer the kid next door.

But Otto was thinking ahead, and he shifted gears. "How's that Aunt Cora of yours? She's sure a *pistol*. I'd like to have Cora come to my place for a nice, long, loving afternoon visit."*Swish. Smack.* Glancing at Derek, I'd been suckered again.

"At least she's not like her weak younger sister, your poor mother who couldn't face the strong world. I'll bet Cora still talks about me and our dates. I showed her a real good time … a real big time."

A wave of anger swept over me as Otto insulted my mother and Aunt Cora. *Swoosh. Thunk.* Geez, fooled again!

"C'mon, James," came from the bleachers. "Keep your eye on the ball. Don't listen to the catcher. He's *trying* to distract you, and it's *working*."

Once again I got into my favorite stance, crouching a little. Otto's voice was just above a whisper: "I hope you and Natalia take after your Aunt Cora, not your mother. Cora clearly got the better genes."

I kept telling myself to *Forget him* as Derek went into his windup and fired another hard one. I swung the bat as hard as I could, but the ball dipped at the end, and I missed. Stepping back, I took a couple of practice swings. Derek had a breaking pitch to add to his fastball, and I adjusted my thinking. My sore left arm kept reminding me *Be Ready. Eye on the ball. Swing quicker.*

When I moved into my stance, Otto muttered, "A pretty boy like you, James, you're just not cut out for manly stuff."

When Derek started his windup, I sensed the ball would be coming high and near the outside corner. When he released the fast one, I started my swing a fraction sooner, giving it every ounce of strength within me, but it all seemed to happen in slow motion. This time I saw the ball rotating as it reached the plate, and I timed my swing perfectly.

The bat made that sweet *crack* players love to hear, and the baseball rose in a majestic arc toward deep left center field. As I finished my swing like a wound-up top, I saw Walt turning, looking up into the cloudless sky, and taking a few steps toward the fence. Out of the corner of my eye I saw the coach and his wife leap off the bleachers like a pair of jack-in-the-boxes as they watched. Adell spilled her Coca-Cola, but she didn't notice, and Coach Spencer yelled, "*What a hit*! What a *hit*! That's *big league stuff*!"

Looking to the outfield, I watched the ball carry high over the fence toward the school parking lot about 400 feet away. Behind the pitcher's box Derek had one hand up shading his eyes as he watched the monster hit. He was frowning. At the same moment I heard "*Verdammt*" from behind me, and the catcher's mitt and plopped down on home plate.

A cool idea seized me, and I dropped the bat and trotted toward first base, taking it slow and making sure I touched the base. Rounding first, I trotted to second, rounded second, kept on moving, rounded third, and trotted toward home. Stepping on the plate, I looked at Otto and cracked, "Let's try that again. This is fun!"

To my surprise, he looked at me and gave me his friendly smile. I glanced out at the pitcher's box, and Derek was rubbing his left knee. He looked in at Otto with a painful expression. In a low voice he said, "My knee is killing me. We need to get back to your place."

Otto was crouched on one knee with a big grin on his chops. "That's enough for today." His voice morphed back to his smooth-as-silk tone. "I'm sure Coach Spencer and his adorable wife will want to collect the gear and head for home."

Surprised, I stared at him, and he reached out one hand. "Help an old man up, James."

Reacting, I helped him. Standing in front of me, he placed one hand on my left shoulder and said in a louder voice, "Just now you were facing a pitcher who is much better than you. We are shaped by our struggles and how we overcome them."

I felt Otto's charm oozing over me like an invisible fog. He continued: "In spite of what you were up against, you didn't quit. Instead, you kept struggling, and finally you lifted yourself to new heights. That special swing was magnificent." Tears appeared in his eyes. "Like your coach said, you took a major league swing at a major league fastball, and the hit that exploded off your bat; would have been a home run anywhere, even at Yankee Stadium."

Listening, I wondered how he could transform his personality so easily. Being close to his face, I caught a whiff of his breath. I could tell he was half-drunk. He must have been drinking before he came to the field, even though he wasn't slurring his words. Ironically, at the moment I noticed his condition, his eyes took on a distant look and his speech became slightly slurred. It was like his articulation control engine ran out of gas.

"I've watched you grow up," he murmured. "I never had a son … soon you will be expected to go overseas and kill good German boys … but maybe not … I'm in the middle of some business now, but when it's over … Derek

will be leaving … I'd like you to come over and watch a
movie with me … got my own projector … it will open
your eyes … not a movie that will ever play at the local
theater … *Triumph des Willens* … *Triumph of the Will* …
that's what you experienced today, James, a triumph of
your *will* …"

Watching him, I didn't know what to say. Without
acknowledging his words, I removed his hand from my
shoulder, turned, and walked away. The coach and his wife
were waiting by the backstop.

"James," Spencer said, grinning. "You're going to
be a star for Jefferson High next year. That booming hit
carried all the way to the parking lot! You brought tears to
my eyes. It reminds me of when I was your age and playing
sandlot ball right on this diamond in the summer."

Amazed, I started to reply, but Adell hugged me.
"You made my sweetheart proud today! I've seen baseball
games on this field for many years, but I never saw a hit
like that!"

They wished me well. Feeling uplifted, I looked
around and saw Walt ambling toward me. Grinning at each
other, we left for home. As we walked off the school
grounds, he elbowed me.

"Wow, James, and I mean *Wow*! While you were
talking to Mister Herman, I ran out to the parking lot and
looked for that ball you hit. There's too much long grass
around the edges, and I couldn't find it." He sighed.
"Buddy, you're gonna be the big hitter on the Broncos this
summer! I can't wait for our first game!"

Smiling at him, I felt secretly like I emerged from the practice a hero. "Walt, I don't know if I can hit that well ever again. You couldn't hear it out there, but Mister Herman was taunting me. He and Derek were deliberately trying to humiliate me, and at first they made me mad. But I got control of myself, tried to ignore them, and give it my best shot."

The rest of the way home we exchanged tidbits from the practice, including the players having Coca-Cola's furnished by Adell Spencer, not to mention Adam hitting his home run. We also talked about girls, and getting a first date. At his driveway, Walt remarked, "You know, James, I figured you'd hit one over the fence, if anyone did, but not that long a blast!" He grinned. "Who knows? Maybe Adam will make the varsity next spring, too!"

We parted there in front of the Bunkers' farm. The next practice was set for Wednesday at 3:00, and the first game would be next Friday at 1:00. Walt waved goodbye as he walked toward the house. His family lives in a two-story Victorian which looks a lot like ours. He's got a kid brother, Dougie, who's ten, and he was waiting in the front yard to play catch. Sometimes I wish I had a brother to play ball with, but that's life. Having a sister has its advantages too, and especially now that we're going to try secretly spying.

The rest of the way home I spent thinking about Otto. He was a Nazi sympathizer, but somehow he had trusted me enough to let his true colors show. Maybe he figured no one would believe me if I tried spreading the truth about his beliefs. Was it illegal to be a Nazi sympathizer? I wasn't sure, but we live in a country founded on principles like free speech and free religion. Even if it wasn't illegal, Otto would be ostracized by his neighbors if the truth about him was known.

At that point it dawned on me that Otto being a Nazi sympathizer didn't necessarily mean he was a German spy. After all, Charlottesville didn't have any war factories, and there were no rumors of the University of Virginia conducting war-related research. What could anyone spy on in Charlottesville? Maybe Otto's immersion in fascist literature had left him a little screwy in the brain like a religious fanatic or the grand wizard in a secret society.

At the front door, I had to admit I felt tempted to see the movie *Triumph of the Will*. Mister Bronston once said it was a Nazi propaganda film featuring Hitler that was created in the mid-1930s. It was supposed to be a fine example of cinematic art, regardless of the film's accuracy. Here in our country the movie was seen as forbidden fruit, but why not have a taste? I could always appreciate the art that went into making the film and reject the propaganda.

As soon as I stepped inside, Nat called out from the kitchen: "You're late for lunch, but we had sandwiches and apples and iced tea. I made you a sandwich and put it in the fridge, and there's tea in there too."

The clock on the kitchen wall said 12:45. Aunt Cora was washing the dishes, and Dad must have been outside working. Nat said, "Dad wants us to weed the vegetable garden, the whole acre, but I thought I'd wait for you to join me." She flashed a smile, because she hates working in the garden. She knows I probably do most of the farm work, and she prefers it that way.

The rest of the afternoon was filled with weeding the garden. After more than an hour, Nat went inside and came out with two bottles of Nesbitt's Orange Soda from the fridge. It must have been close to 4:00 when we finished. We stood under the big oak near the barn, and downed those bottles of soda. She asked me about the baseball practice, and I told her some of the fun stuff, but not about what happened with Otto and Derek. I always thought she kind of liked Walt Bunker, but she never said so.

Since the subject was in the air, I told Nat that Walt and I had a conversation about girls about a month ago. He's got his eye on a certain girl, and I told him I had my eye on Linda Lawton, the slender brunette who's father runs the IGA market in Charlottesville. She will be in the tenth grade, so she's a year behind me. She's got big brown eyes, long brown hair, a sweet smile, and she's kind of shy. On the way home I mentioned to Walt that after school starts again, when Linda's in the 10th grade and I'm in the 11th, I plan to ask her to a dance after a football game.

After I'd told Walt about Linda, he told me a secret. He hasn't had a date yet either, but he said his buddy Jack Jones has a girlfriend, Sallie Redfield. Jack doesn't say much about her, but it turns out they met at three different dances last fall. She let him kiss her once when he was walking her home. The Redfields live in that big Tudor place over on Elm Street. They've got a swing on the front porch, and Jack sits and holds hands with Sallie before she has to go in for the night. Her folks want her home by 10:00 on Friday and Saturday nights, except when there's a school dance on those nights she can stay out until 10:30.

At his house, Walt headed along the driveway, stopped, and looked back. "Remember, James. This is our secret, right?"

"Yeah, relax. I'm not keen on anyone else knowing what I'm thinking either about girls. Who needs all the guys on the team kidding us, huh?" I looked around, but nobody was in sight. "When the first fall dance comes," and I flicked my eyes, "we will see what we see, right?!"

Walt gave me his biggest. "That's us! Yeah, we're gonna *see* what we *see*!"

We winked at each other, and he headed for his house.

I downed the rest of my soft drink, and Nat was staring at me and smiling. I hoped she wouldn't quiz me, and she remarked, "I'm a little surprised, James. I've never heard you talk about girls before."

I just grinned. "Well, that doesn't mean the subject isn't on my mind, you know. Sooner or later, *everyone* thinks about girls. Are you really gonna tell me you *don't* think about boys?"

Of course, she blushed. "Well, I have to admit I like Karl. He kissed me the other day …" When my eyes opened wider, she blushed as red as a ripe apple. "But don't worry, James. I'm still going to get some information out of him about his Uncle Otto. I'll also try to see what Karl knows about Derek Miller, the so-called friend of the Herman family."

"Well, I sure hope so, Sis. I think anyone bold enough to come to Virginia and declare 'Heil, Hitler!' is suspicious, and Karl is staying at the same house. There might be more to us being involved in spying than I first thought."

Nat smiled at me as she turned and headed for the house. I hoped she wasn't going to jump into deep water with Karl, or with Otto. I'll admit that thought once worried me, but I decided to wait and see.

CHAPTER 7: Teenage Spies

Sunday night after dinner, I strolled out to the barn to feed the horses. It had been a nice day, starting with Dad driving all of us, including Aunt Cora, to Charlottesville to attend the 11:00 worship service at Calvary Presbyterian Church. Afterward, he took us to Timberlake's on Main Street. They have a great lunch counter in the back, just beyond the pharmacy. We all had hamburgers and French fries, and for dessert, Dad ordered chocolate custard. We saw a lot of young people there. I guess most of them were students at the University of Virginia. After all, it's only a short walk to the campus.

After taking care of the horses, I headed back to the house. I was going to relax and do a little reading. A few minutes later I was lying on the sofa with a library book when Nat came into the living room.

"Whatcha reading?"

I rotated the book in my hands to check the title. I looked at her, and smiled. "*Final Secret*. It's about the events going on in 1941 and the espionage in Honolulu leading up to Pearl Harbor."

She eyed me quizzically. "How can there be a book about Pearl Harbor? That just happened a few months ago."

"Just part of the spring publishing effort, I guess. In fact, there were two books about Pearl Harbor on the New Acquisitions shelf. I didn't check, but I imagine they're both written by journalists. I asked Miss Martin, the librarian, you know, the smart lady with glasses who likes to talk about her cats. She said there are plenty of reporters, or journalists, if you prefer, who write daily stories about certain events or people, and later, they compile them into books on the same subject. Of course, they've done more research and added new material. Evidently the author of *Final Secret* is an American sent over to cover the story, and afterward he wrote this book. I think a lot of it is autobiographical."

Nat looked at the back cover. "*Wow*! If that's the author on the back cover, I would like to run into him. He's handsome, distinguished, the whole works."

I turned the book around and looked at the image of the author. Oddly, his face reminded me of my own, I mean, when he was younger. There's a definite resemblance.

I thought about teasing Nat about it, but I thought better of it. She already indicated she found the guy sexy. And for me to point out a resemblance, that might come across like me trying to flatter myself. Ah, brothers and sisters! So much to tease about, but you've gotta tread carefully, if you're close in age.

She grinned. "You're going to be an expert on Pearl Harbor, huh?"

I sighed. "Why not? After lunch you and I spent most of today doing chores. Our next baseball practice isn't until Wednesday, and the first game is next Friday. I've got some free time, and I like history anyway."

Looking at her again, I could see the spark in her greenish eyes. "What's up with you?"

She smiled and looked away. "This afternoon I checked with Otto to see when he wanted me to do more cleaning, and of course, while I was there, I ran into Karl. We went for a walk and we talked, and we …"

Her voice trailed off, but I knew she was holding back. "Okay, Sis. Tell me."

"Well, it's a little strange. When we got into talking, Karl told me he was learning German this past year, because the War Department, or maybe it's the State Department, started a program teaching German on a volunteer basis to teenage guys who probably will end up serving in the US Army. It seems they prefer those who have German ancestry, and Karl fits the bill. The general idea is that after the war is won, our Army, along with other countries' armies, will be occupying a defeated Germany.

"So, of course, they'll need as many soldiers as possible to understand and speak German. That way they'll be able to deal with civilians more effectively. Anyhow, Karl said his father used to speak German before his mother died, but after that, he concentrated on speaking English. As a kid, Karl picked up the language from listening to his dad and mother, and with the new classes, well, he's getting fluent. Our government offers classes in Japanese for the same purpose, but of course, he chose German.

"Look, James, listening to Karl gave me an idea. I asked him if his Uncle Otto knows he can speak German. Karl just laughed, and said, 'No way!' When he first arrived, he was going to tell Otto. But he was tired out from the train trip, went to bed early, and never got around to it.

"Anyway, the next morning when he got up, Karl heard his uncle downstairs speaking German with another man. It was the first time Karl heard German spoken in the Herman house. Later, he learned it was Derek Miller, the 'friend' from New York City. Otto said Derek will be with them at dinner tonight, and Karl's idea was he'd surprise them by speaking German."

"Interesting, Nat, but what's your point?"

"Hang on, brother! That's when I had my great idea for *spying*. But I couldn't tell Karl that his uncle and the friend might be Nazi spies, could I? He probably wouldn't believe it."

Her grin was wide, and she continued: "So I said to Karl, 'You could do me a big favor if you don't tell your uncle that you're fluent in German, at least not yet. When I get the meal ready for them on Monday evening, I'll mention that Aunt Cora has asked me if he, Otto, ever speaks about her. She met him when she first moved here, and he's seen her a few times.

"Anyway, my idea is if I ask Otto about her, later he might speak about it in German to Derek. Maybe he'll reveal to Derek whether he has feelings for our aunt. So Karl could listen and, afterward, he could tell me. Aunt Cora would like to know if Otto still favors her. If not, well, we'll drop the idea.

"Guess what?! Karl thought a little innocent spying might be fun. From what he's already told me, I know he doesn't care much for Derek Miller. But he knows Otto is impressed by Derek, so it's better to avoid the subject. So you see, Karl's going to do a little spying tomorrow evening. He thinks he's listening to remarks about Cora, but I'm hoping he'll hear Otto talk about his spy plans. If so, Karl will be rattled. But don't worry. I can get him to tell me what he overheard when I go over there tomorrow."

"Look, Nat, you know as well as I do that Aunt Cora did 'see' Otto a few times, but not recently. Something must have happened between them, because now she seldom says anything personal about him."

"Of course, James. But as long as you or Dad don't say anything about Otto and Aunt Cora, Karl won't know that. And I'm not going to tell him, and mess up the plan."

Shaking my head, I smiled. "Well, I'm not going to tell him. I never cared much for Otto, but if anyone around here is a Nazi, I think he's the perfect choice. Naturally he acts innocent, like he's really a good guy. As anyone who's read any murder mysteries knows, the so-called 'bad guy' is almost always someone who looks and talks like a 'good guy.' Even in the Western movies, the bad guys mostly pose as pillars of the community. That's ol' Otto, isn't it?"

"Of course, James. But I still won't let Karl in on our secret. Look, we could just be *wrong*, as you've told me, and Otto just *might* be a good guy. At least this way we're gonna find out."

Reflecting on it, we smiled at each other. Overall, I had to admit I was impressed by the plan. It's worth taking the chance, and I told Nat so.

She jumped up, grinned, and headed for her bedroom. I opened *Final Secret* and started reading. I've already reached the part where the main character is writing a column for a Honolulu newspaper about events happening in 1941 in Hawaii, the Pacific, and the Far East.

Later, when I closed the book and got up to head for my bedroom, I thought about our plans and said to myself, *Look out, Otto. My kid sister is coming after you*!

CHAPTER 8: Secret Plans

On Tuesday morning following breakfast, I headed to the barn. Dad wanted me to give the floor a once-over and get rid of the straw and dirt. After that, I needed to restack the bales of hay, making room for when we start the new harvest in September. That's Dad for you. He planned ahead and didn't like leaving anything to chance. If you live on a farm, you take care of everything, the land, the crops, the animals, the buildings, and the equipment. Who knows? Maybe after college I'll end up being a farmer. At least I'll know the business.

Nat appeared in the barn about a minute later. I grinned at her. "Good timing! Do you want to help clean the barn? I thought you were going to the market today with Aunt Cora. Dad's out working in the apple orchards."

"We'll go in an hour or so. Aunt Cora's upstairs taking care of something. I didn't get a chance to tell you yesterday, but I worked at Otto's. We've settled on me working a couple of hours on Monday, Wednesday, and Friday, so today's an 'off day.'"

She was anxious to tell me what she knew, so we sat on the carved wooden bench just inside the doors. "Here's what happened, James. Karl told me this when we sat with his arm around me under that big tree yesterday afternoon."

I nodded, and she carried on with her tale: "After dinner, which I prepared around 5:00, I washed the dishes and cleaned the kitchen. Karl gave me a 'knowing' look once Otto and Derek went into the living room. A minute later Karl went into the parlor, where Otto keeps his magazines and books. When I walked past the kitchen entrance with a stack of dishes, I saw Karl paging through the *Saturday Evening Post*. But he had an ear cocked to hear Otto and Derek in the next room. They were sitting on the living room sofa and speaking German, you know, in low voices.

"I stopped and looked at Karl. He saw me, flashed a smile, and turned back to the magazine. I figured it was a signal that he could understand them. I walked back home, ate dinner, returned about 7:00, and went for another walk with Karl. We took our time and walked all the way to the back boundary of our land to that old bench under the oak tree, the one where our mother used to take us."

Nat blushed, but she kept talking: "He told me that when he heard Otto speaking in English about the 'plan,' Derek stopped him and said in German, 'Are you quite sure he can't understand the language?' Well, Otto replied that his nephew didn't know German, because his father quit speaking the language shortly after his mother died. He said Karl was only five at the time, so he 'didn't have a clue.' Those are Karl's words, not mine."

While she was talking, Nat had been watching the brown mare eating hay in the stall. Turning, she faced me. "Otto might think he knows all about what's going on around here, but evidently Derek doesn't trust what he sees and hears, at least not without Otto's say-so."

"That's interesting, Sis, but is there more?"

"James, just *relax*." She flicked a quick smile. "Karl told me he thinks his uncle *must* be spying for the *Germans*. Karl's father, Lionel Ellis, is a chemist. From what his dad told him off the record, just before the summer trip, he's part of some secret group of scientists in New York that will be researching new weapons. Some of them are physicists, but they have a whole bunch of scientists involved. He said one time his dad mentioned a 'Manhattan Project.' But right afterward, Mister Ellis told him to forget he ever heard that name."

She paused, and her greenish eyes were bright. "Okay, James, here's where it gets *really* interesting. Karl was also surprised to hear Uncle Otto and his friend Derek talking about 'secret weapons research,' and that's a quote, going on in New York. And guess what? Karl also heard them say his dad will soon be told he *must* pass secret information to them."

Nat rolled her eyes. "Next you'll wonder why he would do that, right? Well, the answer is simple. Mister Ellis will be told if he doesn't cooperate, he'll never see Karl *alive* again."

She stopped and looked away for a few moments, before facing me again. "See, if Mister Ellis does agree to spy for the enemy, his reputation and career would be ruined, and he could even be sent to *prison*. Maybe even worse, he might give the enemy valuable information." She sighed. "So, he'd really be over a barrel."

"Hold on, Sis! If what you're saying happens, we'd need to help Karl. You're telling me he could be an innocent victim in this secret spy stuff." I shuddered. "I'm beginning to be sorry we ever heard of Otto Herman."

When I turned to Nat, she had her face buried in her hands. Her body was trembling, and I knew she was crying.

That's when I knew she had fallen in love with Karl. I started to wonder what the two of them were up to, but instead I placed my hand on her arm to offer a little brotherly love.

In a few moments she sat up straight, pulled out her handkerchief, and blew her nose. Returning the hanky to her pocket, she wiped her eyes with one hand. "That's not all, James. Karl heard his uncle say the man in charge of the spy stuff, so-called *Comrade X*, is out of town. But when he returns, Comrade X will make the first approach to Mister Ellis. Karl's dad will be asked to deliver detailed plans on the secret project, or the Nazis get *tough*. Otto plans to take Karl to a cabin up in the mountains where nobody can find him. But Otto doesn't own the place. He just rents it from a friend. So his name isn't on the title, meaning the government would have a hard time finding it. Nobody, except Otto and Derek, would know where Karl was being held."

She looked at me, and her eyes got teary again. "When he was telling me, Karl broke down for a few seconds, so I hugged him to show I believe him. I might have kissed him once or twice too, but never mind that."

Stopping for a moment, she took a deep breath. "Anyway, the big plot involves Otto taking Karl to this secret cabin a day or two *before* Comrade X threatens his father. Derek is supposed to keep an eye on the farm as well as on me while he's gone. If anyone asks, Derek will say Otto is away on a *business trip*."

She peered at me with frustration in her eyes. "Don't you see, James? That means Karl's father will have to turn against the US government, or risk losing his son.

"Otto said if all goes well and Mister Ellis gives the information to the Nazis, Karl will never even know he's been held hostage. Otto will bring him back to the farm, and Karl will spend another few weeks helping out, doing chores, and maybe seeing me."

She grinned awkwardly. "But Karl confided to me that he just *can't* let this happen. He's going to run away tomorrow, but he told me so I wouldn't wonder where he went. But of course, if anyone asks me, I'll just say I really have no idea."

Again Nat sighed. Glancing at each other, we looked around the barn. The horses were munching straw like everything in the whole world was fine. Besides the horses, the main sound we heard was a barn owl up above making an occasional *screech*, kind of like a tool scraping glass. I looked up, and that owl was sitting on a beam in the middle next to another brown owl. They looked down at us with their big black eyes.

Nat didn't see the owl. She had her head in her hands, and I just left her alone. I thought about Karl, and I'll admit I did wonder about him at first. But evidently he was soon to be used as a pawn in an evil international plot. After a while Nat sat up, wiped her eyes, and looked at me.

"Listen, James. I want you to hear this firsthand."

Before I could reply, she jumped up and hurried toward the house. I watched her walk around the right side. A few seconds later she reappeared, towing Karl by one hand. In a few moments they reached the barn doors, and Nat said, "Come inside, Karl. We don't want to be conspicuous."

I stood up and we formed a little triangle in front of the bench, out of sight from the house. Grinning like a fox, Nat asked if I had questions. Having thought about it, I was ready. "We need to get in touch with the authorities, the Albemarle County sheriff or the Charlottesville police."

Karl shook his head. "Please, we can't do that. If we do, it might cause my father to lose his job in New York. It might even destroy his career as a chemistry professor."

I shook my head. "Think about it, Karl. We've got to act like patriotic Americans. If we don't, when it all comes out, which it will sooner or later, we're going to look bad. But if your father betrays the US while he's working on a government project, he's not only going to be facing prison, but he might be facing execution. I say we *have* to go to the police."

"James, wait!" Nat looked at me with fear coloring her eyes. "Otto has cronies in the county sheriff's office and with the town police. You and I have both seen police cars several times at his drinking parties. That's partly why he gets away with everything. He's got friends in *law enforcement*. If we accuse him, Otto will deny it and probably even make a joke out of it. So who will people believe, a popular neighbor, or some teenagers?"

Immediately I saw her point, and my mind was racing. We looked at each other for a few moments, and a light blinked on in my mind. "*Okaayy*, you two. We can't trust this secret spy information to a phone call. Let's take a bus to Richmond tomorrow. In Social Studies this year, our book mentioned the Federal Bureau of Investigation has an office in each state capital. I can find the address in the Telephone Directory."

I could feel my excitement growing. "Otto *can't* influence the FBI. They're America's national police force, and I know they will listen, even if we are teenagers. Karl's story is real, and he can name names. Let's face it. The spying you're talking about could affect America's war effort. The FBI will *have* to listen to what we know on that subject."

Nat interrupted. "I like the idea, James, but we need a pretext, you know, a *reason* for the trip."

I grinned at them. "Quite correct, and I know a reason that Dad will buy. We can take the bus to Richmond and supposedly see the Richmond Colts baseball game. They play in the Class B Piedmont League, and right now they're in third place. Their home games are at a new ballpark, Mooer's Field. We can look up the address. Heck, I read about the Colts everyday in our newspaper!"

Nat quickly agreed, and Karl, who didn't know much about life in Virginia, figured any way he could get away from his uncle was the answer. After we rehashed the ball game plan, I went inside and called the Trailways Bus Station. The woman who answered told me the first bus to Richmond left Charlottesville at 8:25.

Back in the barn, I told Nat and Karl what I had learned. After more talk, Karl left for his Uncle Otto's. He promised to be back in the morning by 7:30 so we could walk into town and be on time at the bus station. I telephoned Coach Spencer to say I'd be out of town on a trip tomorrow, so I wouldn't be at baseball practice. He said okay, we'll see you at our game on Saturday. He knows I can play first base, left field, and swing the bat.

That night at dinner I brought up the subject, and Dad's reaction was to smile and agree. He likes the Colts, too. But Aunt Cora said, "Won't it be dangerous for teenagers to travel all the way to Richmond on a *bus*?"

Dad, who has good memories of when he played baseball, just looked at her and chuckled. "They'll be okay, Cora. I took more than one bus trip to Richmond before I turned sixteen. They'll be fine."

Nat chimed in about Karl, saying he wanted to go with us. Again Aunt Cora looked skeptical. "Won't his uncle miss him doing his chores?"

I kept quiet, and Nat said, "We told Karl about the idea today, and he went home to do extra work this afternoon. I'm sure Mister Herman won't mind."

My sister gave Aunt Cora a sweet smile, and she dropped the subject. In a few minutes we finished dinner, and Dad announced the new *Reader's Digest* came in the mail, and he was going to read it.

He stood up, smiled, and complimented Aunt Cora on the fine meal. We had pot roast, green beans, mashed potatoes, and, of course, her home-baked bread. Dad headed for the living room. When Nat started helping Aunt Cora with the dishes, I took off for my bedroom. As I was climbing the stairs, I heard Nat carrying on a lively conversation to placate our aunt.

In my bedroom, I checked my savings. I had just over $52, and I kept the bills and coins in a little red lock box that Dad once gave me. I took out four $5 bills. I thought that should cover the cost of the bus, the baseball tickets, and lunch at a restaurant. As I placed the bills in my wallet, I had second thoughts. I fished out a $10 bill, just in case, and tucked it in the secret compartment. Choosing a blue shirt and my gray church trousers, I hung them carefully over the chair next to my bed. Under the chair I placed my black shoes.

Half an hour later Nat came floating up the steps, and I could tell she was excited. Her smile must have stretched ear to ear when she peeked in my room. "Are you getting ready, James? We haven't heard anything from Karl. He'd telephone us if his uncle wouldn't let him go."

I shrugged. "Oh, I figure good ol' Uncle Otto won't mind. After all, he's supposed to be a pillar of the community and a good guy. As long as the leaders in New York aren't ready to squeeze Karl's dad for secrets, Otto will be good to his nephew. Still, we need to make this trip right away. Coach Spencer didn't mind me missing tomorrow's practice. Everyone knows I like the Colts. Heck, Spencer would probably go, if he had the chance. Anyway, he knows I'm good enough to start, so it can't hurt to miss one practice."

We both felt very good. Nat left to get cleaned up, take out her clothes for tomorrow, and I picked up my library book. I am getting really interested in Pearl Harbor and the events of 1941.

CHAPTER 9: Richmond and the FBI

I sure had my fill of riding a bus by the time the Trailways coach pulled into the Richmond Depot just after 10:00 on Wednesday. Since Nat, Karl, and I bought our tickets that morning, we ended up occupying the back bench. The trip took a little over an hour and a half. Highway 250 was paved all the way from Main Street in Charlottesville to Broad Street in downtown Richmond, so the ride was fairly smooth. But I'm glad we don't have one of those leather-backed benches in our home. My legs felt a bit wobbly as I stepped down from the bus.

Nat and Karl came right behind me, and I could see the excitement on their faces. Heck, I was excited too! This was my first trip to the state capital, and I looked around in awe. Men and women of all ages dressed in every imaginable way, along with a few kids in nice clothes, were hurrying in every direction. Cars honked, brakes squealed, and traffic cops dotted every intersection. Before leaving home, I looked up the FBI's headquarters in Charlottesville's phone book. I knew the agency's address, but we needed directions. I held up my hand to stop a stout man with a top hat, a cane, and a black bulldog on a leash.

He peered at me with dark eyes set in a fat face with a gray handlebar mustache. The bulldog snorted. For a moment they made me think of a chunky walrus led by a squat bodyguard.

"What do y'all want, sonny?" He sounded like a character from *Gone with the Wind*. "Cain't y'all see we're in a hurrah?"

Thinking quickly, I bowed. "Yes, sir, and I hate to bother you." I glanced at Nat and Karl, and they were gazing at his wrinkled dog. "We've traveled here today from Charlottesville with an urgent message to be delivered to the FBI at Seventh and Main Streets. Could you point us in the correct direction?"

Again I bowed. He glanced suspiciously at my friends. Then he smiled, making his face wrinkle like his dog's. Waving his arm, he pointed ahead. "Y'all just follow this sidewalk and make a right in three blocks. Look for the Richmond Trust Building. The big doorman's going to show y'all where to go."

Thanking him, I smiled. The bulldog sniffed at my black shoes, its nose twitched, and the owner said, "C'mon, Buddy. These young folks are busy too." Nodding, he strolled away.

Nat grinned as the bulldog's owner disappeared into a department store. "Let's go, James. We need to talk to the federal agents." She grinned at Karl, who hadn't said a word since leaving the bus. I knew he was nervous, because his information might soon be investigated.

I followed Nat and Karl, watching the well-dressed men and women who ignored us as they moved ahead on their own business. I'd never seen so many men wearing suits, mostly brown and black and gray. Many of the women wore fancy dresses, dress hats, and high heels, and they walked as fast as the men. For a few moments I watched a grizzled man sitting against a building and holding out a tin cup. He was saying "Hi, y'all!" to each person who passed. Beside him sat a brown hound dog with sad eyes staring at me. I shuddered. Pulling a quarter from my pocket, I dropped it in the cup. The man said something, and I hurried to catch up with Nat and Karl.

After turning the corner, we saw on the other side of the street a multi-storied brick building with a granite arch around its double glass doors as well as granite ledges and crowns framing the tall windows. When a uniformed policeman with white gloves whistled and waved at us, we hurried across the four-lane street. Looking impressive with his peaked cap and neat blue uniform, the cop winked as we passed.

I smiled at him, and for some reason his gesture gave me a lift. On the opposite corner, I said to Nat and Karl, "I'm taking the lead. Stick with me, listen to the agents, and make mental notes."

Grinning, Nat nodded, and I approached the stocky doorman. A dark-faced guard with large brown eyes and thick lips, he looked important in his fancy red uniform trimmed with gold braid. His eyes followed me like a cat after a mouse.

I looked up into his round face. "Sir, we were told the FBI offices are in this building, the Richmond Trust Building." I paused while he studied us, his gaze darting from me to Nat to Karl, and back.

"Yezzir! You done come to the right place." His face lit up like a lamp being switched on, but then he rubbed his chin thoughtfully. "You kids, y'all *sure* you gotta see the FBI? Them folks, they're always busy, see?"

Looking at him, I saw Sammy Baxter sewn in gold over his chest pocket. I explained our business, and when I finished, Nat spoke up. "Sir, we've been riding the bus all the way from Charlottesville. Like my brother says, we really *must* see the FBI. We know we can *trust* them."

Sammy smiled, exposing bright white teeth. Clearing his throat, he declared, "Go on inside, then. Go to the last teller's window on the left. The lady workin' there will call upstairs. In a while an FBI agent will come and meet you. Look for a kinda impressive fellow wearin' a blue suit, a red necktie, and a white shirt." He winked. "And don't be surprised if his black shoes don't *shine* like the *sun*!"

He chuckled, giving me a warm feeling. "You're maybe gonna meet Mister Becker."

Leaning forward, his voice took on an important tone. "The agents, 'member, they're busy. You wanna get right straight to the point, see?" He winked one eye slowly, pulling himself to his full height.

We walked into a gray-walled, high-ceilinged lobby. Behind the customer waiting area with half a dozen chairs, we saw four teller's windows on each side of the room. A stout uniformed guard with a military bearing watched us from his post beside the first window. I noticed his right hand rested on the handle of a pistol in a leather holster hanging on his black belt. It made me shudder, and I thought, *These people are serious*. Behind me Nat whispered, "They can't think we're crooks, *can they*?"

We reached the last window with its vertical bars. Placing my hands on the ledge, I smiled at a stiff-faced, gray-haired woman wearing a gray suit and wire-rimmed glasses. The brass plaque inside the cage read Miss Smith. As we looked at her, she focused her black eyes on me and spoke in a stern voice: "Do you have *official* business, young man?"

She darted her gaze back and forth between Nat and Karl like they were out of place. Clearing her throat, she observed airily, "I'm *quite* busy today."

Later, I concluded she presented the picture of stiff-necked efficiency for those who might bother FBI officials. When I explained our business, she studied me with her dark eyes. Perhaps feeling the woman's hesitation, Nat pushed her face close to the cage. "We just *must* see an agent. It *really* is a matter of life or death. And we still must ride that rickety bus back over the old highway to Charlottesville. We *most certainly* would appreciate your help."

Nat smiled sweetly, and Miss Smith's tight lips slowly morphed into a thin smile. Picking up the black telephone receiver at her elbow, she dialed a numeral. As she stared off into space, we waited for several long seconds. Suddenly she blinked. "Yes, I have some young people who may have a problem that merits the agency's attention." She looked at me, and her eyes seemed warmer. "Yes, sir, of course."

Hanging up, she stated, "Wait right here. Do *not* leave this area."

We stepped to one side, and looked toward the two elevators with tan metal doors on the right side of the rear wall. Each door was topped by a polished granite ledge and a semicircular floor indicator with a black needle. One needle pointed at 3 and the other at 4. Glancing at Miss Smith's window, I saw nobody waiting. It dawned on me that she wasn't a bank teller.

Somehow I felt amused, but at that moment the left elevator doors parted, an operator pulled back the flexible metal gate, and a tall business type in a blue suit stepped out. Hesitating, he peered in our direction. He came striding forward, keeping his eyes focused on us.

Arriving, he displayed a bronze oval-shaped badge with "Bureau of" in an arc across the top and "Investigation" above an eagle carrying arrows in its claws. "Department of Justice" was across the bottom. We were still staring at the badge when he pocketed it.

"Follow me," he said. An inch or two more than six feet, he had black eyes, crewcut black hair, and an athletic build. Turning on his heel, the big agent walked rapidly back toward the same elevator. We followed him, walking faster to keep up. We went after him into the elevator, and he looked up at the intricately-decorated wooden ceiling like it was a puzzle. The operator, a short middle-aged man in a gray uniform with red trim, white gloves, and a peaked cap looked at us through small brown eyes. Without a word, he pulled the accordion gate closed, pressed a button, and the outer doors slowly closed. He pulled a lever, and the elevator lifted slowly upward until we bumped to a stop. Facing us, the operator stated frostily, "Third floor."

The doors opened, the tall agent in the blue suit walked out, and we followed him along a marble corridor with pale blue walls. Nobody else was in sight, and the brown doors to the offices on both sides were closed. At the end of the hallway, he stopped at the last door on the right. Knocking twice, he paused, and knocked twice again. After a few moments, he pushed the door open. A pleasant voice said, "Come in, please."

In the center of the square office with yellow walls we saw an ornate oak desk with a stack of files on one side and two black telephones on the other. Seated behind the desk and watching us was a good-looking woman with blond hair, wide blue eyes, and an oval face. I thought she could have been a fashion model. Approaching the desk, we saw a brass plaque identifying her as Miss Brown. Smiling sweetly, she pressed a button but kept her big eyes on us. I wondered if she had a pistol concealed in the top drawer, maybe as a last line of defense against enemies disguised as citizens.

In a few moments the door behind her opened, and a tall broad-shouldered man in a blue suit appeared. Perhaps six-foot-two with his brown hair styled in a crewcut, he apprised all three of us with darting brown eyes. Nodding, he motioned us inside. We walked slowly around the secretary's desk and entered what felt like the inner sanctum of the FBI. On the wall behind the dark desk hung a framed picture. My eyes were drawn to the portrait of a round-faced man with dark eyes in a blue suit with his blue tie knotted neatly. He peered at us like suspects. It was Director Hoover himself. I glanced at Nat and Karl, and they were staring at the picture.

The strong voice grabbed our attention, and we faced its owner. "I'm federal agent Henry Becker. Take these seats, please." A line of three straight-backed chairs sat in front of his large desk with its brass fixtures. As Becker lowered himself into a captain's chair, I sat in the first chair, Nat took the chair next to me, and Karl sank slowly into the last one. Out of the corner of my eye I could see Karl looked as pale as a man facing a trial or punishment. I studied Becker.

The big agent had a craggy face, a wide chin, and a dominant manner. His eyes pierced my thoughts like spears. What came to mind is *He's the US government. I sure hope our story is going to be important enough for him to help us.*

"Miss Smith downstairs indicated your business may be important." Becker moved his solemn gaze between us. "But let's hear it in your words." He looked at me. "You look like you're in charge, son. Tell me your name and the purpose of your visit."

At that moment the blonde secretary appeared. She took up a position at the rear corner of the agent's desk, and gave us a sweet smile. She had a pen, a stenographer's pad, and a floral air about her. For a few moments, I looked at her engaging eyes. My cheeks flushed, and at that moment our mission felt overwhelming.

Drawing a deep breath, I stated my name, James Edward Baker. I explained that Otto Herman, our neighbor outside Charlottesville, seemed cheerful enough to neighbors and friends, particularly to those who came to his drinking parties. I knew his background was German, but I said we had never heard him speak German, until recently. Then I covered the afternoon when my sister Nat and I went to his house to deliver two bags of potatoes. When nobody answered the door, we walked around the side of the house. When we heard voices through a side window, we ducked below the ledge. Otto was talking with someone my sister later identified as Derek Miller. At one point Miller declared quite loudly, "Heil, Hitler!"

I turned to Karl. "Why don't you tell him what you told us yesterday?"

Agent Becker looked him over. "What is your name, young man?"

"I'm Karl Ellis, and I live in New York City." Taking a deep breath, he tried to smile.

Becker eyed him. "Why did you travel here to the agency today?"

Karl looked embarrassed, but he continued: "I came with my friends here," and he glanced at us. "I'm visiting my Uncle Otto Herman, who lives outside Charlottesville, for a few weeks from New York City. He is my deceased mother's brother. My father is a chemistry professor at NYU. Right now he's on leave, and he's working as a chemist on a secret government research project in New York, well, actually in Manhattan …"

Becker held up his right hand. "Are you sure the project is in Manhattan, not somewhere else in New York City?"

"Yes, sir," Karl replied, and I could see his nervous look. "The one time my father did tell me about his work, kind of in a general way, he called it the 'Manhattan Project.' I could see in his eyes he made a slip, and right away he told me to *forget* I ever heard that name. Well, that scared me."

"Hold on, Mister Ellis." Becker looked surprised. Frowning, he turned to Miss Brown. She must have been taking notes in shorthand, because her pen was flying over the page. She nodded, and he turned back to Karl.

"What comes next will be off the record." Miss Brown, raising her eyes, nodded and lifted her pen from the notebook.

Turning to us, Becker said solemnly: "The Manhattan Project is strictly top secret. I know about its existence, but I know none of the details, and I wouldn't tell you if I did. However, you are no longer innocent teenagers, but you are soldiers on the home front. What is required of you is adult levels of discretion, good judgment, and absolute loyalty."

All three of us did a collective *gulp*, and nodded at the agent like our heads were linked together.

Becker turned back to the secretary. "Okay, Miss Brown. You may resume."

He focused his gaze on Karl. "Okay, Mister Ellis. Please continue with your story."

Nodding once, Karl gave a brief summary, indicating that he was able to hear the conversation between his uncle Otto and Derek Miller because they didn't know he could speak German. From what they said, he learned that a group in New York led by a man called Comrade X planned to blackmail his father for information about the project by threatening to kidnap him.

Karl glanced at Nat. "Instead, I decided to leave Charlottesville, and maybe return home, so my uncle or his friends couldn't kidnap me. That way they couldn't blackmail my father. But I realized if I returned home, well, I could be kidnapped from there."

Karl lowered his eyes, maybe to conceal fear, but in a moment he said, "When I went next door to tell Nat, because I didn't want to take off without telling her, she and her brother …" and he nodded at us. "They convinced me to come here to Richmond and report what I know to the FBI."

Karl was finished, and I mean literally finished, because relating his information to a federal agent seemed to have drained him. He lowered his head, and his body trembled. I could see tears on his cheeks, and Nat clasped his hand. He looked at her, managed to grin, and the tears stopped.

Raising his head, he looked again at Becker. "I'm sorry, sir. I'm afraid something's going to happen to my dad, and I just want to do the right thing." Again he lowered his eyes. For a few moments silence hovered like a dark cloud in the room. Becker glanced at the secretary, and she nodded. "Miss Smith will go now and type your notes in the form of a statement, Mister Ellis."

The big agent watched the good-looking secretary stride to the door on her high heels, open it, and leave. When the door clicked closed, Becker turned back to Karl. "When your statement is finished, you will need to sign it."

I was hanging on his every word, and out of the corner of my eye, I could see Nat and Karl were doing likewise.

Becker turned to me. "The agency will develop a plan, Mister Ellis. Your father will be protected. Also, we will send more than one agent to Charlottesville, secretly, of course, to maintain surveillance on Otto Herman."

He paused. "I may get involved myself. In any event, you three," and he moved his eyes between us, "have acted correctly today by giving us cause to believe the security of an important project in New York may be threatened. You must return to Charlottesville and act as if you enjoyed your time in Richmond."

I leaned forward. "Sir, Nat and I told Dad, and Karl told Otto, that we were riding the bus here to see a Richmond Colts game.""Very good, Mister Baker. But let's check on that." Smiling, Becker picked up his telephone, dialed 0, and listened. "Please find out what's happening in today's game with the Colts. I need to know if they are at home at Mooer's Field."

Agent Becker looked at us impassively, and we waited. In a few moments the phone buzzed, he lifted the receiver, and listened. "Yes, I see. Thank you." He dropped the receiver into its cradle. Studying us, he said, "The Colts are out of town today. Do you have a Plan B?"

Nat spoke up. "Not yet, but I have an idea. I've read about The Valentine, the museum here in Richmond that has all kinds of pictures and artifacts about Virginia History." She turned to me. "That's where we're going, right after we eat lunch!"

Becker nodded, and from his top drawer he pulled a pamphlet. "Take this, Miss Baker. This booklet tells about the features of The Valentine. Normally you can only purchase these at the museum." He pushed it across the desk, and Nat eagerly took it.

"Last but not least, Mister Baker." The agent pulled a card from his suit coat pocket, wrote on it, and handed it to me. "This is my personal card. If you are questioned or threatened by Otto Herman, call me. This number will reach me at any hour. When someone answers and asks for the code, you say 'Colts,' understood?"

I nodded eagerly, and the agent added, "Keep the card with you."

With a smile, Becker stood up. I took the cue, got to my feet, and Nat and Karl followed suit. I looked at the big FBI agent, and I knew he'd be a tough man for an opponent. I smiled.

Becker raised his eyebrows. "Why are you smiling, Mister Baker? Do you like the museum idea?"

"I'm smiling, sir, because I'm glad the FBI is gonna be on our side!"

I glanced over at Nat and Karl, and both were looking relieved. I knew they were happy too.

I thought Becker winked once before he walked briskly to the door, opened it, and led us into the outer office. He indicated the secretary's desk, Karl stepped over, and she handed him the typed document. He read it, took the fountain pen she offered, and signed his name carefully at the bottom. Becker took the document, looked it over, and turned to Miss Brown. "Please call agent Johnson and ask him to come up here. He will escort these fine young people downstairs."

As the secretary dialed a number and spoke into her telephone, Becker turned to us. "You will hear from me, possibly in a day or two. You are *not* to talk about our meeting today to anyone. Is that understood?"

He peered at each of us, and we all agreed. "Mister Baker, I will communicate with you, and to you, Miss Baker, and I will speak with your father. He needs to know that his son and daughter are at risk." He eyed me. "If he says 'No,' the agency will try something else."

Becker looked at Nat. "I hope you can find a way to talk with Mister Ellis when you're at the neighbor's farm, but without arousing suspicion."

Nat smiled. "My idea is I will pretend like I'm Karl's *girlfriend*." Glancing at her, Karl blushed, but he didn't speak. I knew my sister could pull it off, but I knew she had more than *pretending* in mind. She was in love, and I smiled. In a few moments the office door opened, agent Johnson beckoned, and we followed him downstairs. The day looked brighter when we walked outside.

CHAPTER 10: Kidnapped

On Friday around 11:00, two days after we returned from Richmond, Nat left to do the cleaning and housework for Otto. We had our first game that afternoon at 1:00 at the high school, and I could hardly wait. Following a light lunch, I walked to the high school field. Walt must have left before me, because I didn't see him along the way.

The weather was sunny and warm with a slight breeze blowing out to left field. The Broncos and the Vikings took turns using the diamond to warm up. Standard practice is for the visitors to use the field first to take infield and outfield and a few swings of batting practice. The home team would start by playing catch and doing the batting and fielding drill "pepper" on the sidelines. Afterward, the teams would exchange places and reverse the procedure. As usual, pepper included the exchange of

friendly comments and wise cracks, but all in good spirits.
Most of us knew each other, at least from classes at
school.For this game the Broncos were the home team, and
the game went all the way to the seventh inning before I
batted for the fourth time. So far I was hitless. Their pitcher
was Carl Hillman, a junior right-hander who wore glasses,
mixed his pitches well, and sometimes played outfield for
the varsity. He had already fanned me twice. The third time
he gave me a low outside fastball, and I connected, but my
high fly ball was caught by the center fielder.

When I came to bat in the seventh, we had one out.
Herb Jenkowski led off with a smash up the middle, but
their tall shortstop, Mike Good, managed to snag it on one
hop and make a swell throw for the out. Walt Bunker batted
next, and he looped a single down the left field line. After
him, Jack Jones swung a little late on a Hillman fastball,
but he lined a double into deep right.

Walt stood out there, hands on hips, peering at me
from third, and Jack was leading off at second. Hillman
went through his slow wind-up and nearly fooled me with a
big curveball, but I had watched him throw mostly
fastballs, and this time I guessed 'curve.' When he used
more of a sidearm motion, I focused on the curve as it
began to break. Timing it just right, I took my short stride
and swung hard. Everyone could hear the *crack* of the bat,
and Boy! That ball soared like a small white rocket high
over the chain link fence in left center! By the time I
rounded third, all the guys were clapping and yelling and
jumping around, so we won in our last at-bats!

Afterward, walking home with Walt, I basked in the
glow of a slugger. I'll admit the feeling was a new one for
me, but the more I thought about it, the more I knew
improvement and experience accounted for my hard but

level swing. Walt kept teasing me about being the "next" Babe Ruth, but I could only grin. Later at dinner, which we finally started around 6:30, I told Dad and Aunt Cora about it. Dad understood about improving one's swing, because he had lived through the slow process many years earlier. He also looked quite pleased to hear about my game-winning homer. Still, I didn't miss his occasional glances at Nat's empty chair.

For some reason she had not yet returned from Otto's farm and her Friday housework. At least three times Dad reassured Cora that Nat probably had extra cleaning to do, and she would be home soon.

My father and my aunt knew about Nat seeing Karl on the days she wasn't helping at the Herman house, and they knew the two of them were taking long walks together. Nat mentioned it once, and Dad didn't seem to mind. Evidently he thought it was fine for his 14-year-old daughter to have an older boy interested in her. However, he didn't know that Karl was kissing Nat.

But I knew the real story about her and Karl, including our bus trip to see the FBI in Richmond. Afterward, we spent an hour at The Valentine museum, and Nat brought home the pamphlet given to her by agent Becker. Actually, the long bus ride home turned out to be no big deal, because the three of us couldn't stop talking about how to proceed with what Nat dubbed our "Herman Problem."After dinner, Dad got up to go into the living room and read. But he reached the dining room entrance, stopped, and glanced at his watch. Looking at me, he motioned me to join him. We strolled into the living room and sat on our red mohair davenport.

"Look, James," he said, keeping his voice low. "I don't want to upset your aunt, but I'm wondering about Nat." He checked his watch again. "It's 7:30, and she's never stayed over there after 6:00. She knows that's when we usually eat dinner, and she knows Cora goes out of her way to have the meal prepared on time." Pausing, he gave me a worried look. "If your sister isn't home by 8:00, I want you to go and check. If she's *that* involved with Karl, then something's up, and I need to talk to her." He studied me for a few moments, the worry showing in his blue eyes. "Understood?"

"Sure, Dad." I nodded, and my mind was racing. "I've been wondering, too."

I almost blurted out the spying gambit, but I didn't. I figured Dad would be mad at me for not telling him sooner about the FBI. I was caught on the horns of a dilemma, so I kept it to myself.

Nodding at me, Dad picked up the latest *Saturday Evening Post* off the coffee table, and I stood up, stretched, and headed up the stairs to my bedroom. Taking off my shoes, I grabbed my library book and started to read. But knowing Dad was worried about Nat's whereabouts made me more concerned. I made it through a few pages, but I caught myself rereading some of the paragraphs. I couldn't really concentrate, and my eyes kept returning to the alarm clock beside me. Finally, when the hands reached 7:55, I couldn't wait any longer. I hopped up, laced on my shoes, grabbed my flashlight, and moved quietly down the stairs.

I could hear Aunt Cora talking to Dad in the living room about stuff like the grocery prices being too high and President Roosevelt doing nothing about it. I tiptoed to the kitchen, slipped out the back door, and moved down the steps. I looked over in the direction of Otto's house, but in the twilight I couldn't see much. The corn was thriving in our field between the two houses, and the stalks were about five feet tall. I decided to sneak through the corn rather than use the road and walk along Otto's driveway. A voice in my mind was saying *Be careful*.Reaching the field, I parted the stalks and placed my feet carefully, trying not to break any. In five minutes I reached Otto's side yard. Once there, I hustled over the damp grass until I reached the large oak that offered so much shade in the daylight. Stopping beside the tree, I listened. I couldn't hear any sounds. It was nearly dark, but I couldn't see lights inside the house. I looked out at the barn. Somewhere inside a light was turned on, maybe near the horse stalls.Something didn't feel right. I debated whether to go back and tell Dad, because he was smarter and stronger than me. As I stood there thinking, I looked back and forth between the house and the barn. Suddenly it hit me that after Derek arrived, two cars were usually parked at the end of the driveway. Tonight his blue Dodge was gone.I headed for the front porch, took the two steps in one stride, and started to knock on the door. As I raised my fist, I noticed the door open a crack. That was odd. I pushed it open further, and the darkness seemed to pull me like a magnet. I stepped inside and looked around. No lights were burning, and I couldn't hear a sound. In the distance I heard a horse whinny, but that was it.

Switching on my flashlight, I said, "*Hello*! *Hello*! Is anyone home? This is James. I'm looking for my sister Nat, because she didn't come home for dinner."

In the silence my voice seemed louder than usual. As I stood there, the house had an abandoned feeling. All of a sudden I felt chills running up my spine. I moved over to a floor lamp, and pushed the switch. Nothing happened.

There was no electricity! I felt sick to my stomach like I had eaten something rotten. I shined my flashlight around. "*Natalia?* Are you *here*?" Again, no reply, so I started searching. The inside of Otto's Victorian looked similar to the layout of our house. There was a good-sized living room with a davenport and easy chairs. The parlor had chairs, bookcases, and a pile of magazines. The small dining room had a table, chairs, and a china cabinet. In the large kitchen were a refrigerator, an electric stove, and a long wooden table surrounded by chairs. There was also the back room that Otto used for his office. I walked slowly through all the rooms, except the office which was locked. I kept shining my light here and there and calling her name. I found nothing, not in the kitchen pantry, not in the rooms, not in the bathroom, not in closets, not anywhere.

Shuddering, I knew I had to look upstairs. The staircase with its banister was situated beside the dining room, and the wooden steps were carpeted. I climbed them slowly, and the second tread creaked ominously. Ignoring it, I kept moving. At the top of the stairs, I followed the beam of my flashlight into four bedrooms, the closets, and the half bathroom. Again I found nothing. Returning downstairs, I was scared. At the same time I was calling my sister's name, my mind was saying *What happened to Nat*? I kept expecting a muffled cry for help, but not a word came.

I opened the basement door, but all I could see was cobwebs above the stairs and all over the railings. The smell arising from the basement was dank and musty like inside a cavern. I called her name, but no reply. It looked and felt like nobody had used the basement in ages. Turning around, I headed for Otto's office, the only room with a locked door. Gripping the flashlight tightly like it was a valued friend, I placed my ear against the door and listened for a long minute. I heard nothing, and I knew nobody was in the house. It made me tense.

Moving outside, I closed the front door, descended the steps, and walked around the house. I tried to shine the light in the rear window that I knew must be Otto's office, but the glass was opaque. It looked like someone had painted the inside of it a dark color. It was one more oddball thing about Otto. I knew I had to head for home and tell Dad.

Overhead a crescent moon was rising in the east. The day had been sunny and clear, and now a million stars twinkled in the heavens. Switching off the flashlight, I trudged along the driveway to the road and on to our house. In no time I reached the back door, and went inside. The kitchen light was on, but it was empty. All the dishes and flatware had been washed, dried, and put away for tomorrow. I wanted to talk to Dad privately. When I reached the entrance to the living room, I saw he was still on the couch, a magazine on his lap, but his head was resting against the back.

As I walked slowly toward him, Aunt Cora, sitting in the blue easy chair with her knitting in her hands and her basket of yarn on the floor, warned, "You shouldn't wake your father. He's had a long, hard day."

I glanced at her. "Sorry, I've got to wake him up."

Sputtering, she made a nasty comment, but I ignored it. Leaning over, I touched his arm. "Dad, wake up. Something's *wrong*."

Behind me Cora gasped. Opening his eyes, Dad sat up with a start. For a few moments he seemed dazed, but then he nodded. "Sit down, son. Tell me what's bothering you."

My stomach felt sick, but I sat beside him. Taking a deep breath, I looked into his worried eyes. All of a sudden the words just tumbled out of me. I told him about our trip to Richmond, our visit to the FBI offices, and our meeting with agent Henry Becker, and, just now, my search of Otto's house. Of course, he and Aunt Cora were horrified about the Herman house being dark and empty as well as Derek's blue car being gone.

Dad focused on me, and I expected the worst. Instead, he asked calmly, "You have a number for this agent Becker, correct? And you're *sure* nobody is at Otto's house?"

I don't know how he kept so calm, but that was Dad. He didn't panic in a crisis. "Positive," I replied. Still, the thought that I shouldn't have accepted the spy idea kept nagging at me."Son, we're going to call this federal agent, and I mean *now*." He glanced at his watch. "It's past 9:00." He stood up, and we headed for the wall telephone in the kitchen.

"*Zeke*," came Cora's trembling voice. "This whole thing is terrible! James needs to be punished, and I mean *severely*. You need to …"

Stopping in the doorway, he turned and peered at her. After a few moments, he stated, "Cora, I will take care of this situation with my son and daughter, and I do *not* need advice."

Her mouth dropped open, and she began to reply, but evidently his stern reply gave her second thoughts. In the kitchen with Dad, I took out my wallet and found the card from Becker. It looked like any other business card with his first and last names, the address of the Richmond Trust, and a hand-written telephone number.I handed the card to Dad, and he looked it over. "This doesn't say FBI on it." He eyed me. "Are you *sure* this man is legitimate?"

"Well, he didn't take out his badge, but Mister Johnson, the agent who came to the lobby and led us to the offices on the third floor, did show us his bronze badge. I saw it, and I'm positive it's real. Inside the head agent's personal office, I saw the picture of J. Edgar Hoover on the wall. And Mister Becker listened to us quite carefully, and his secretary took notes."

As Dad was standing there considering my reply, the telephone rang like a firebell in the night. He glanced at me, and picked up the receiver. "Hello … Yes, this is the Baker residence." His eyes opened wider, and he silently mouthed the word *Becker*.

Adrenaline rushed through me, and I felt my excitement rising. Agent Becker had promised to call soon, but he must have been delayed. I watched as my father listened intently, and behind us I heard Aunt Cora enter the kitchen. "Zeke, let me …"

Turning, he glanced at her and held up his hand like a traffic cop. I swear his eyes said *Back off*. Again he listened. It felt like we waited for an eternity, but it was just a few minutes. At one point my breathing became so rapid that I felt dizzy, but the feeling faded.

Looking at both of us, Dad said, "Yes, sir. It seems my daughter Natalia and Karl Ellis, a nephew of Otto Herman, have both disappeared today." He paused. "My son James tells me a fellow named Derek Miller was visiting from New York, and his car is gone."

He lowered the receiver. "Do we know the license number of the Dodge?"

I took a deep breath, closed my eyes, and thought for a moment. A happy feeling spread inside me because I remembered it, or at least most of it. "There is an 'N' and three digits. There is something in front of the N, but I don't know what. The three digits after the N are 4-0-6. I noticed it in the first place because .406 was Ted Williams' batting average last year!"

With the receiver back to his ear, Dad repeated what I said. In moments he smiled. "Yes sir, we will look for you bright and early tomorrow morning."

Thanking the agent, Dad returned the receiver carefully to its cradle like it was our only lifeline to the world. Maybe that night it was.

Looking at Cora and me, Dad smiled. "FBI agents will be in Charlottesville by dawn tomorrow. They will take care of notifying the Charlottesville police, the Washington, DC, police, and the police in New York City."

This time I saw tears in Dad's eyes, and Aunt Cora saw it too. She crossed the room and hugged him. They hugged each other for a long time, and I could see her crying. I closed my own eyes and said a prayer. I felt my cheeks getting wet. Somehow, some way, I knew we were going to find Nat and Karl. I made up my mind to do whatever I could to help.

Dad released Cora and hugged me. Backing up a step and holding me by the shoulders, he said, "Maybe you shouldn't have gotten into this so-called spying, but maybe Karl and Nat would have been kidnapped anyhow. At least now the FBI is on the job."

He turned to Cora. "I'll be up at 5:00 tomorrow, so let's have breakfast at 6:00. It will be the longest day of our lives."

Turning, he headed for the living room. I took the cue, left Aunt Cora alone, and practically glided up the stairs. As I sat on the bed in my quiet bedroom, I knew my father really loved us. A feeling of relief washed over me like a large wave at the seashore.

Later, when I drifted off to sleep, I dreamed of being Superman and swooping down on Otto and Derek. I would dispatch each one with a mighty blast from my fist. I was floating over Charlottesville when I drifted into a cloud, and I don't remember any more.

CHAPTER 11: The Search

That Saturday morning our house felt more like a circus than a farm. Fortunately, we had gotten up early, dressed, and finished Aunt Cora's breakfast of eggs, bacon, toast, and coffee. I normally drink milk, but I had coffee too. Shortly after 7:00, while I was sitting on the davenport looking at *Time Magazine*, a double knock came to the front door. Dad and Aunt Cora were cleaning the kitchen, but they practically flew into the living room. I opened the door, and there stood FBI agent Henry Becker with four other men. He lifted his navy blue Stetson by way of greeting.

"May we come in, please?" Without waiting, Becker led the way inside for his law enforcement colleagues. Acknowledging us, they formed a line just inside the door. Shaking hands with Dad, Becker introduced himself first. "I'm Henry Becker, in charge of the Richmond Office of the Federal Bureau of Investigation. We are here largely because of your son's and daughter's courage."

Reaching into his blue suit coat, he retrieved a bronze FBI badge and held it out. Dad glanced at it, nodded, and Becker grinned. Looking at Aunt Cora, he bowed slightly. "Ma'am, good morning."

Dad was impressed, but Cora looked worried. Turning to his partners, Becker introduced William Johnson, the tall agent we met in Richmond. Next to him stood Gary Russell, a trim six-footer with brown hair who wore wire-rimmed glasses. Gary smiled at Dad. "It's good to see you, Zeke. It's been too long since we last got together."

Surprised, Becker looked at Dad and then at Russell. "You two *know* each other?"

Dad chuckled. "Yes, we played baseball and football here in high school. I lost touch with Gary when he moved to Richmond. I heard he worked for the FBI, but …"

"Good enough," Becker said, indicating the others. "These two men are detectives with the Charlottesville Police Department." He introduced Lieutenant Able Stanislas, who was a fiftyish six-footer with brown eyes, crewcut brown hair, and the *I've seen it all* look, and Sergeant Harold Dexter, a bit shorter than Stanislas with a blond crew cut and a slight lisp when he spoke.

Both detectives stepped forward and shook hands with Dad. Stanislas, the more formidable presence, said, in his deep voice, "Sergeant Dexter and I will do what we can with the FBI and, of course, your family, sir. You should know Harry and I have worked on *more* than one kidnapping."

Stanislas rolled his eyes when he spoke as if he should be in charge. Personally, I thought the FBI was our best bet, and I trusted Becker after meeting him at FBI headquarters.

Becker ignored the sarcasm and turned to me. "Tell these officers what your friend Karl Ellis heard Otto say to Derek Miller at the Herman farm."

Nodding, I spent several minutes depicting Otto and recalling what Karl told us. I concluded with my summary of searching the house last night, and finding it empty. I mentioned that Otto's office was locked, and the window was painted on the inside. "I wasn't sure about what to do, but I thought the FBI and the police would know."

Stanislas looked at me. "I fail to understand why Otto Herman, a German, wouldn't think his nephew could understand German. After all, didn't the kid's father come from Germany too?"

His question threw me off balance for a moment, but after glancing at Becker, I replied, "Karl told us that his father used to speak German at home, until his mother died when he was four or five. After that, he said his dad dropped using German and concentrated on speaking English. Mister Ellis is a chemistry professor at New York University, so maybe he believed it would be easier for students if he spoke English without an accent."

Stanislas seemed satisfied, and Becker asked, "Anyone else have any questions?" When nobody spoke, he turned to me. "James, is there anything else you can tell us that might help find your sister and your friend?"

I wasn't going to say it, but I decided not to hold back. "Aunt Cora was seeing Otto for a while this past year …"

"Yes," Cora interrupted. "I *can* add something."

Suddenly everyone's eyes turned to my aunt. Dad started to speak, but this time she held up her hand to stop.

"I'm a widow, and I have been for six *long* years." Tears came to her eyes, and she paused. "I dated Otto several times during the past year, but not for the last few weeks. Mostly he would drive us into Charlottesville, and we'd eat at a nice restaurant. I cook a lot, you know, so it was a treat. Anyway, Otto was *always* friendly and charming. And he's big, strong, and funny …"

She wiped away her tears with a lace hanky. "A couple of times we went to a Saturday afternoon matinee at the Jefferson Theater. Of course, we'd go for dinner afterward."

Cora took a deep breath. "Now, the last time we got together, it was different, *very* different. On a Saturday morning he drove me up to a cabin in the mountains around here. I'm not sure where it was, but it took an hour and a half."

Again she paused, looking thoughtful. "You know, he did say an *acquaintance* owned the cabin. Anyway, that morning he drank what he called a Manhattan before we left home, and he took the bottle of whiskey with him. So, at the cabin he had a few more. The place was sort of rustic, but his drinking made me nervous. I didn't say anything because I was afraid to make him *mad*."

Shaking her head and frowning, Cora carried on: "In his shiny black Oldsmobile on the way there, I didn't pay much attention to the roads. I was mainly enjoying the scenery, you know, and, well, listening to his stories while he did the driving. But coming home, we took a different road, and I remember it. I'm pretty sure it's state highway 48. Anyway, I did the driving, and I stopped for gas at the S&H Grocery, which is near a town called Schuyler. You see, I *had* to drive home, because Otto had *too much* to drink, and I was afraid he'd get us in an accident."

Suddenly she burst into tears, and her cheeks flushed. Her whole body shook. I knew she was embarrassed, and probably ashamed, because it was pretty obvious Otto took her to the cabin for a little making out. After a few moments, Dad saved the day. He stepped over and hugged her, and nobody spoke. Finally she said, "I'm okay, *really*."

Dad smiled at her, and backed away, and Aunt Cora wiped her eyes with her hanky. Afterward, she took a deep breath. "Okay, then, once we got off the mountain, the whole trip to Charlottesville took about an hour. By then Otto had fallen asleep on the front seat beside me, with his head kind of slumped back on the seat. Well, we finally came to his farm. I parked that black Olds in the driveway, got out, and left him sleeping, you know, in the car."

Shaking her head, she grinned. "Ever since, you know, I just make some excuse if he asks me to go out for dinner or a movie. Otto simply is *not* the nice guy he *pretends* to be."

Dad had been listening carefully, and he asked, "So Otto actually got too drunk to drive?"

"Yes, Zeke. I *know* when a man's drunk. My Joe used to get that way, well, once in a while." She wiped a hand across her forehead like telling the story had exhausted her, and maybe it did.

Agent Becker was listening carefully, and he focused his brown eyes on her. "Think, Ma'am. Is there anything else you remember about that trip, like the road leading to the cabin, or anything, no matter how small the details?"

Aunt Cora looked off in the distance for a moment, and suddenly her face lit up. "Well, the road going up the mountain was the usual two lanes. But once we got close, we turned off on a narrow dirt road, and we drove slowly for a while, and then we turned into a *narrower* dirt track, and that one took us through the woods to the cabin. At the entrance to *that* dirt road, I noticed a rusty old *mailbox*. I didn't see a name on it, but the mailbox was kind of tipped over sideways, you know, like somebody beat it with a club. Anyway, the mailbox was all but falling *off* the post."

She gave Dad a quick smile, and Becker looked at agent Russell. He was taking notes, and he nodded. Russell didn't miss the new details. I smiled and thought *Good for you, Aunt Cora.*

Becker huddled with the agents and the detectives. In a few minutes they decided to send two unmarked cars to Schuyler, and starting there, search the nearby mountains. Lieutenant Stanislas figured the mountain they were looking for had to be Afton Mountain. I noticed Sergeant Dexter kind of shook his head, but he said nothing when Stanislas stared at him.

Becker said Dad would travel in his black sedan along with agent Russell, while Johnson, the other agent, would drive along with Stanislas and Dexter in the other car. When I asked about me coming along, my father said in no uncertain terms that I was *not* going, period. I was to stay with Aunt Cora and make sure everything went smoothly here on the farm.

"Besides," Dad said, "you're playing for the Broncos, and you can't let down your teammates."

Lieutenant Stanislas borrowed our phone to call his office, and the others went outside to prepare for the trip. I listened to a lot of palaver about where the cabin was and on which mountain, and stuff like that. Half an hour later, Officer Harris from the Charlottesville Police arrived with two road maps.

At that point Aunt Cora left for the kitchen, but she wouldn't even look at me. I knew she blamed me for the kidnapping. She didn't need to do that, because I already blamed myself. I walked out to the kitchen for a drink of water, and Aunt Cora was hurrying around and making sandwiches for the men to take. Dad came in and filled his canteen with water. Of course, he noticed the chilly atmosphere. Glancing at me, he went over to Cora. He put his arm around her, hugged her, and spoke quietly. Out of the corner of my eye, I saw her nodding.

Just then Lieutenant Stanislas and agent Becker walked into the kitchen for water. Stanislas looked at Dad. "Mister Baker, I sent Sergeant Dexter and Officer Harris over to Herman's house. Your boy never got into that locked office, so I want them to break in and look for clues about where Otto Herman and Derek Miller might have taken the captives."

Becker growled, "Stanislas, you shouldn't have done that *without* consulting me. I'm directing this operation, and I thought about doing the same thing. However, I figured his office might be rigged …"

I was standing at the window with my glass of water and looking toward Otto's house and listening to them. Before Becker could finish, we heard a huge *BOOM*. I saw the flash of light even before I heard the explosion. Immediately the house burst into flames, and a big cloud of smoke billowed above it. Except for the movies, I've never even seen such a sight!

We rushed out the back door and into the yard. The officers already outside seemed dazed for a moment or two. Agent Russell was shaking his head and pointing to our elm tree. The tree was split down the middle like a bolt of lightning had struck it. Inside the crack was wedged the flag pole that used to be hanging from the front porch of Otto's house. The explosion blasted that flagpole up in the air, and it fell down at our elm like a javelin. The windows of our house facing Otto's house were cracked, but somehow the kitchen window where I was standing was spared. Reflecting on it, I thought *Maybe this is my lucky day*.

I was standing next to Russell when he turned to Becker and observed, "In case we were wondering, that bomb tells us Otto Herman left home with no intention of returning."

About that time umpteen scraps of scorched paper began floating down in our yard like a rainstorm of confetti. I picked up part of a page that had the printed title *Unite for a Jew-free America!* Dropping it, I found part of the front of a pamphlet called *Franklin Roosevelt's Communist Roots*. The law enforcement guys were making remarks about the same stuff, Dad was shaking his head, and Aunt Cora was crying.

After a few minutes, Stanislas led the police officers through the cornfield to check on the house. I heard brakes, and I saw another police car in our driveway. Two officers jumped out, and the first one asked where the lieutenant was. Dad told him, and they took off like jackrabbits, running through the cornfield. Later, an ambulance arrived, and the agents who went to Otto's place to check the damage had returned. They told the attendants to wait a while, just in case. I heard Becker tell Dad, "They can only find body parts. Your neighbor Otto Herman is a Nazi, no question about it. And he's vicious as well as dangerous."

It was late morning before the two cars full of grim-faced men left our farm. Dad rode with Becker and Russell in one black unmarked Ford sedan; while Johnson, Stanislas, and two other officers rode in the second black car. I heard Becker telling them that the men would need to scour the mountains near Schuyler and find that cabin, no matter how long it took. Firemen from the Charlottesville Fire Department were waiting in a car out front of Otto's place. They would check through the remains of the house, once the ruins cooled off.

I busied myself nailing pieces of plywood over our side windows thinking we could replace the glass later. Aunt Cora was so outraged by the mess of paper and the vile writing that she got a burlap bag out of the barn and started picking up each and every piece.

I was thinking about hurrying, but I really had nothing else better to do. I was on the stepladder nailing the last corner of the plywood on the second window when she came and stood beside me.

"James! Come down here and *read this*!"

Forgetting my thoughts, I backed down the ladder, and she handed me a charred pamphlet. Unlike most of the scraps, this booklet was intact. It even looked professionally printed in color. The title was *Alpine Retreats in America for Aryan Youth*. The picture under it showed two Boy Scouts in uniform standing in front of a cabin made of vertical wooden timbers. The cabin was in a scenic mountain setting, and behind it some distance away was a rushing blue waterfall.

"*That's it*! Aunt Cora declared.

"What's *it*?" I looked at her.

"That picture reminds me of something about the cabin where Otto took me. Behind it, there's an outhouse. The yard back of the cabin sort of slopes down toward it. Not ten feet behind the outhouse, there's a big dropoff. You can stand up there and look over the valley. The valley's pretty much covered with trees, and across the valley, over on the far side you see a pretty waterfall spilling out over some rocks. The water gushes and falls more than twenty feet. Do you think that piece of information might help the agents and the policemen?"

"Yes, I sure do!"

I hugged her long and hard, and when she pulled away, I could see tears glistening on her cheeks. She was still an attractive woman with her wavy brown hair, big brown eyes, the nose like our Mom's, and she still had her figure. I could see why Otto would be interested. But as soon as that thought hit me, I got mad at Otto all over again. He was a kidnapper as well as a Nazi. I went inside, grabbed the phone, checked my FBI card, and dialed Becker's number.

"Hello, Federal Agent Becker's office. Who's calling, please?"

I gave her my name and told her that I needed to get a message to agent Becker whom I knew was in his car driving to the mountains near Charlottesville. The operator said she had not been able to reach him all morning, but she would give him my message just as soon as contact was made. I told her my message was urgent, thanked her, and hung up.

I knew Becker and his partners were heading for Schuyler and the mountains, and he'd have to find a Bell Telephone booth to call his office. I walked around the yard for a half hour, and I kept glancing over at the wreckage where Otto once lived. Finally, I went inside and called Becker's number again. But once again the operator told me she had not yet been able to reach him.

As I hung up, a plan was forming in my mind. Aunt Cora objected when I told her I was going to drive out in the mountains myself and look for a cabin with a back yard that overlooked a waterfall. I assured her I would come back home, once I ran into the police or the FBI.

I left her frowning at me and hurried upstairs, two steps at a time. In Dad's bedroom I found the keys to his old black '36 Chevy pickup lying on the dresser. Pocketing the keys, I had another bright idea. I remembered that I once saw him stash his Smith and Wesson revolver in his dresser. Bending over, I pulled open the bottom drawer. Sure enough, I found the gun in a box under some folded work shirts. Looking it over, I remembered the wooden grip and four-inch barrel. I took half a dozen bullets from the box, loaded the S&W, and shoved it in my belt.

Feeling full of confidence, I went downstairs, walked outside, and around behind the barn where the old black truck was parked. I climbed in, pulled the choke, and started the six-cylinder engine. It coughed to life and then rumbled like a jungle cat. Placing the gun on the seat, I smiled to myself. As I drove along the driveway, I saw

Aunt Cora standing on the front porch. She had a forlorn look on her face, and for a moment I braked. Looking at her, I waved instead of turning around.

Regardless of being fifteen, I figured my reason was good enough to join the hunt. I was the one who let the spying ball get rolling, and now I had an additional clue. I was determined to stop Otto and his Nazi friend. I shifted gears, headed out the driveway, and drove toward town. For the first time in my life I felt like I was doing a man's job.

CHAPTER 12: My Search

I passed through Schuyler about 4:30, and a few minutes later I arrived at the S&H Grocery with the gas pumps that Aunt Cora had talked about. To avoid questions, I stashed the revolver under the seat. A teenager in a yellow cap with a corncob pipe stuck in the corner of his mouth hoisted himself out of a wooden chair beside the store's screen door and ambled my way. Reaching the window, he looked at me with dark eyes.

"So bud, whaddaya want?" Sucking on the pipe, he blew a stream of smoke from the opposite corner of his mouth like a furnace was burning inside.

"Give me two bucks worth of regular, all right?"

He nodded, moved to the Standard Oil pump, removed the truck's gas cap, and shoved in the nozzle. He turned the crank a couple of times, returning the amount last sold to zero, and squeezed the handle. I got out, and he glanced at me but kept pumping. Half a minute later, as I watched, the numerals behind the glass reached $2.00. He withdrew the nozzle, inhaled on his pipe, blew more smoke, and jerked his thumb at the store. "Pay granddad inside." Replacing the nozzle, he followed me until reaching his chair, where he plopped down.

Inside, I looked around. The store had several counters with rows of canned goods with vegetables, fruit, and soup, boxes of cereal, cake mix, baking soda, and more, bottles of everything from ketchup to vinegar to honey, a rack with several kinds of bread, and the like. A stocky man with bushy gray hair, gray eyes, and haggard skin watched me like a hawk. As I walked along the middle aisle, the worn boards squeaked under my black tennis shoes. Over in the corner stood a big red floor cooler with Coca-Cola emblazoned on the lid. It was humming like a top. I took two Clark Bars from an assortment of candy, grabbed a bottle of Coke from the cooler, and popped the cap with the opener.

At the counter stood the elderly owner in his blue-striped overalls. He picked up each candy bar, looked at my Coke, and punched keys on the brass cash register. As he watched me, a voice from outside said, "$2 on the gas, Gramps." The owner's eyes twinkled, his smile showed a couple of teeth missing, and his stubby fingers banged the keys again. Behind him the head of a buck mounted on an overall wooden plaque glared at me with eyes like black marbles. Shuddering, I handed him a five dollar bill.

"Thank you, sonny," he said, and his breath laced with cigarette smoke and yesterday's dinner hit me like a slap. I nodded, took the $2.75 in change, and he grinned. "So, where ya headed?"

I explained I was looking for a cabin in a valley near Afton Mountain.

"Well, where's the cabin, sonny? Afton Mountain's pretty durn big, ya know. There's bears living up there, too" Stopping, he chuckled. "Bears, ya know, they like the taste of kids!"

I ignored the bad joke. "Actually, I don't know for sure where it's located." I grinned hopefully. "But I've seen an old picture of it. The cabin's on a mountain side looking out at a peaceful valley with lots of trees and a high waterfall. The place looks isolated like it's in the wilderness."

Nodding, the old-timer scratched his grizzled chin. Beside him an old brown hound raised its head and turned sorrowful eyes on me. The dog sniffed the air, licked its chops, and flopped its head back down on the boards. *Some dog*, I thought.

"Well, see, there ain't too many cabins like you're talking about up there on Afton," the owner said. "Most of the folks who used to live there, ya know, they've gone and moved to Schuyler, or somewheres else. But there's a coupla valley like what you're describing." He gave me a sly look.

"It just so happens, sonny, I got maps of the area where you're probably gonna look. Of course, I sell 'em for a *quarter*." His gray eyes were shining. "You buy one, and I'll show ya where ya oughta go."

I wondered if he was conning me, but I flipped him a quarter. He snagged it like a sure-handed shortstop. "Hokay, then."

Nodding, he pulled a small map out of the cash register drawer. Taking out a stubby pencil, he spread out the map and put an X on four spots. "I can't be 'exactly sure, but from what you said, these four's gonna be yer best bets."

I walked out with my map, climbed in the driver's seat, and started the pickup's engine. I looked at the map, turned around, and took the two-lane paved road eastward toward the mountain. Three quarters of an hour later I passed over the crest and began cruising down the other side toward Rockfish Valley. It seemed like the road was getting worse, and the uneven surface was pockmarked with holes. I steered carefully for what seemed like half an hour. All at once I came to a wooden board painted with black letters for *Elmer's Emporium and Gas*. Again I decided to stop and ask for help.

Pulling up in front of the ramshackle building with its sloping shingled roof, I parked and stepped out. A dusty black Model T Ford was parked beside the "emporium." In front stood a single Mobilgas pump with a sign displaying the flying red horse. Sitting in a hand-hewn wooden chair by the store's door was a thin boy about my age. His face was freckled, his hair a ginger color, and his eyes small and brown. I noticed his bare feet were dirty. The long weed he was chewing bounced up and down like a bobber with a fish on the line. I looked around, but no one else was in sight.

He stood up, and I noticed the rope in place of a belt around his patched Levis. His white tee shirt had several holes like an animal had chewed it. "Y'all want some gas?" He studied me with his small eyes.

"No, but I'm hoping for directions. Are you Elmer?"

Naw. I'm Cecil. Elmer's my daddy. But, see, he's off fishing, somewheres."

Listening, I noticed a rusty bucket nearby that likely was filled with bait. "Look, Cecil, I'm James. My sister's been kidnapped, and I believe she's being held somewhere near here in a cabin on the mountain."

He nodded, his eyes opened wider, and the weed bounced a little more.

"The only thing I know is the cabin sits above a valley, and the back yard slants down to an outhouse, and then there's a big drop off, and you can see a waterfall in the distance."

Cecil grinned, flipped away the weed, and pulled out a pack of Luckies. He lit one with a match struck on the building. Inhaling, he turned up his head and blew a lopsided moving smoke ring.

He nodded, his nose twitched, and the smoke floated away. "It ain't no valley, it's a ravine. It ain't no waterfall. It's water running downhill from a stream around plenty of rocks, and it's a fair ways back of the cabin. I know the spot, 'cause I was up there fishin' a while back."

I was surprised. "You've been there?"

"Yeeaah." He removed the cigarette, tipped up his face, and blew another smoke ring.

"Maybe a couple weeks back this big, ol' fella in one of them black Olds-mobiles, he stopped and asked if I knew anyone who'd cut down the grass and weeds 'round his cabin. He looked like he didn't know nothin', but then quicklike, he's all smiles, and offers me five bucks. Well, 'course I agreed. So then he rattles off the directions. So, the next day I got out daddy's pickup, and I drove up there, and took me a scythe, and 'course my little brother Vernon too. He's eleven, see. Vern, he did most of the work, and me, being the thinker, well, I took a nap in the truck."

The toothy smile almost wrapped around his face. "Coupla days later, this same big fella with the kinda mean blue eyes, he drove through in that big ol' long Olds, and whaddaya know? Well, he thanks me, and forks over another five, this time all in dollar bills. So, I gave one buck to Vern, and 'course I pocketed the rest." Another broad smile followed, and his eyes twinkled. "I got freckles, so I can't be out in the sun too long. See, our Maw, she always says that."

I chuckled. "Can you describe the man?"

"Oh, I dunno. He's big, *real* old, like fifty, or somethin', with that ol' blond hair, and with a gut on him. And, oh, yeah, he talked kinda funny-like."

"You mean he spoke with an accent?" I eyed Cecil. "Like maybe the Germans speak?"

He squinted. "Yeah, sure, could of been one of them rotten Nat-zees."

At that moment two shots rang out in the distance, and it startled me. Cecil offered the toothy grin. "Prob'ly a hunter poppin' one of them pesky squirrels. There's a bear around here, too." Stopping, he listened. "He prob'ly got him with his second shot."

Nodding, Cecil gave me directions to the cabin. Thanking him, I asked for a favor. "Listen, there's two cars full of lawmen riding around here looking for my sister and for the big blond man's nephew. My sister's fourteen, and he's sixteen. My father is riding in one car. If the cars come by here and stop, will you be sure to tell them about the cabin where I'm heading?"

Watching him, I added, "Tell them James drove off to that cabin, and *please* give them the same directions you gave me."

He eyed me. "Might be I could, but it'd be really nice to give me a ree-ward."

I dug in my pocket and pulled out the change I had from the S&H. I handed it to him, and he squinted. "Ain't much of a ree-ward, huh?"

"Cecil, when we get those captives back and come off the mountain, I promise I'll stop here and give you a real reward. My Dad will, too."

I looked at him closely, and he started drawing circles in the dirt with a big toe. He looked up at me. "Bet you got a gun, huh? I mean, nobody's goin' after a dirty ol' kidnapper with no gun."

He gave me a savvy look, and I nodded. I hurried over to the truck, pulled the S&W from under the seat, and returned. I handed the .38 revolver to him. He looked it over, and his brown eyes glittered like stars. "So, what's it to shoot?"

"It's a .38 Special."

"Well, we got coupla boxes of these bullets, down under the counter. The boxes are kinda dusty, since we ain't had no call for .38's in years."

"Okay, Cecil. When we come back with my sister and my friend, I'll give you this Smith & Wesson."

"Yeah, so … you makin' me a *promise*?"

"Yes, I promise. It'll be yours."

He nodded, went back to drawing circles with his toe, and I climbed back in the pickup.Starting the engine, I followed the new directions toward the cabin. After about half an hour on the gravel road, I took the specified right turn onto a bumpy dirt road. I motored along slowly, going fifteen or twenty miles per hour, and checking the woods on both sides for a smaller dirt road. After a while, I came to a lane, really just a pair of tire tracks, that looked like the one Cecil described. Turning into it, I slowed to about 10 mph. The lane wound like a snake through endless trees. Feeling like I was lost in the woods, I wondered if I'd made a wrong turn.

Suddenly I reached a clearing, and fifty yards ahead could see a small wooden bungalow painted blue with a roof covered with dark shingles. The place had a green door made out of upright wood planks and a pair of windows with white curtains. Reflecting for a few moments, I didn't recall Aunt Cora mentioning the place being *blue*. Turning around, I drove slowly back to the dirt road and the new directions.

A few minutes later I came to another dirt lane leading into the forest. Braking, I spotted a rusty mailbox surrounded by weeds, and it was tilted to one side. That was Aunt Cora's best clue. I smiled and thought *I found the hideout*.

All of a sudden I heard a hissing sound as steam spurted from under the truck's hood. Climbing out, I raised the hood. The radiator was steaming, but after thinking a few moments, I realized what I had to do. Looking in the truck's bed, I found the pail Dad carried for that very purpose. Grabbing it, I looked around, listened, and heard a faint gurgling sound back in the trees.

Smiling to myself and carrying the pail, I made my way slowly through the dense growth of maple, oak, pine, and hickory trees. Once I almost stepped into an animal's burrow, but I reacted in time and moved my foot over it. Passing a mighty oak, I came to the creek. Water was bubbling around rocks of all sizes and shapes. On the other side, a large deer stopped drinking, raised its head, and looked at me. In a flash it turned and disappeared into the trees. Ignoring that, I found a flat rock beside the stream, knelt down, and scooped myself handfuls of water. It tasted fresh and felt cold! After scooping enough water to half fill the bucket, I slowly wound my way back through the forest to the truck. I kept an eye out for wild animals, and maybe a bear.

At the truck, I smiled because the radiator had cooled. Unscrewing the cap, I raised the bucket and slowly poured water into the radiator, until it spilled over. I replaced the cap, dumped the rest of the water, stashed the pail, and climbed back in the driver's seat.

I started the engine, waited for a few moments, and shifted gears. As I turned into the lane, I stopped. *That wouldn't be very smart* I thought. *If Otto's there, he'll hear the truck coming.*

Reflecting, I got a better idea. I drove maybe a hundred yards beyond the lane. Slowing down, I pulled the right front wheel off the road, and parked. I knew sooner or later the FBI and the police would learn from Aunt Cora that I left with the truck to search by myself. Of course, if and when Dad saw the pickup, he'd realize I must be nearby. In fact, maybe anyone else would think the driver was in trouble. I was in the middle of nowhere, and any driver would have to walk some distance to find help.

Climbing out, I hid the keys under the seat on the driver's side, pulled out the revolver, and opened the cylinder. I spun it around to make sure all six bullets were loaded. Satisfied, I shoved the gun into my belt, left the truck's right door open, and headed, as FDR once declared, for my rendezvous with destiny.

CHAPTER 13: Mountain Showdown

After I walked back to the lane, I looked up at the sky and wondered what time it was. I had no wrist watch, so I guessed it was past 6:00. The sun was on the far side of the mountain, the trees were tall, the light in the forest was shadowy, and the shadows seemed to be expanding like ghouls in a bad dream. I walked slowly along the dirt tracks in case a car should approach from the unseen cabin. For a moment I stopped, and tears came to my eyes. What if Nat and Karl were already dead? After all, Otto placing a bomb in his own house proved he could be vicious. He and Derek could have taken my sister and her friend out of state. Wiping my eyes, I wondered where the FBI and the police were searching.

"Well, James, you can't change any of that, can you?"

The words startled me, until I realized it was my voice. Reaching in my belt, I gripped the handle of the S&W. It was too late to turn back. The urge to save Nat and Karl felt like an engine pulling me forward, and again I began walking slowly. I kept pausing, hearing bushes rustle and twigs crack, but I didn't see anyone, so again I would move forward.

After covering maybe a quarter of a mile, I stepped around a large maple, and I saw it. Reacting, I slipped back behind the tree. Waiting a few seconds for my breathing to slow, I peeked around the far side of the maple. The "cabin" wasn't what I expected. It was a small, dilapidated house made of clapboards with the white paint chipping off. The low peaked roof was covered with rough wooden shingles, and a few were missing. The place looked small, maybe two or three rooms.

A pine door and a blue-curtained window faced me. On the right side facing several tall oaks, I could see two more windows with blue curtains. A light was shining through the window on the front and the first one on the side, but the second was dark. Behind the little house, a narrow yard sloped down maybe a hundred feet. A decrepit outhouse sat near the yard's end. Ten yards behind it the ravine began. Across the ravine I could see a narrow steam falling a few yards over the rocks, before it wound its way downhill. The entire scene looked pretty much like Cecil described it. I had to grin.

Again I peered up at the sky. I guessed an hour of semi-daylight remained, but I couldn't wait for total darkness to sneak up and peek inside the window. Leaving the cover of the large maple, I crept slowly through the woods to a thick oak, maybe ten yards away from the right side of the house. Pulling out my gun, I counted silently to three, and ran across the yard as quietly as possible. Within seconds I reached the house, but my heart was beating like a trip-hammer. I closed my eyes, took a deep breath, and waited until my breathing slowed.

I slipped next to the side window with the light showing. The heavy curtains were parted a few inches, and I peeked in. Only part of the room was visible. I saw Karl seated at a long pine table with his back to me. Several lengths of rope crisscrossed the back of his chair, and the rope kept him sitting upright with his hands behind him. Sitting a few feet behind the captive on an old brown couch, I saw Otto relaxing and reading a newspaper like it was Sunday afternoon. I peeked a little further. On the adjacent side of the table I saw Nat seated very tightly against the back of a chair with ropes crisscrossing her waist. I couldn't see her hands, but from the stiff position of her arms, I concluded her wrists were tied in front of her. I couldn't see Derek, and I pulled back.

Thinking about him, I realized he could be out in the woods or in the lane checking to see if anyone was looking for them. Then a horrible thought hit me. If Derek walked along the dirt road, he might find our pickup truck. In the glovebox he'd find the registration for Zeke Baker. If so, he would hurry back and warn Otto.

I looked between the curtains again, and at that moment Derek appeared. He was holding a pistol in his right hand and a bottle of beer in the left. He stopped beside Nat, set down his gun, and grabbed her chin, trying to force her to take a swallow. She clamped her mouth shut, shook her head, and glanced toward Otto. The motion caught his attention. He glared at Derek, and, with his face a bit flushed, he barked something in German. Derek frowned, but he released her, and stepped away. He finished off the beer in the bottle, and wiped his lips. A couple of minutes later, Otto stood up, dropped the newspaper on the sofa, and walked to my right out of sight.

After he left, Derek set his bottle on the table. Grinning like a fox, he moved close to Nat. He kept the gun in his right hand, but his left hand was free. Placing his hand on her shoulder, he slowly reached down into her blouse. She uttered something like *Ohhhh,* and I could see tears forming on her cheeks. Karl had no choice but to watch, but he said something loud. Straining at the ropes, he stood in a crouch, but the ropes made the chair rise with him and kept his hands behind him. He spoke in German with a *pleading* tone. I realized Derek must have been making advances on my sister all day, and my body trembled. I gritted my teeth, closed my eyes, and mumbled a short prayer.

Opening them, I saw Otto reappear. He shoved Karl roughly down, making the chair creak on its legs. Turning, he jerked Derek's hand away from Nat, roaring in English, "*Not yet, fool*!"

Derek said something in German, but he obeyed. Glaring at Otto, he went to the couch and flopped down, with his legs sprawled. He shoved the gun in his pants pocket, all the time staring at Nat like a blue-eyed predator. I considered the problem for a few moments, thinking I could push the front door open, step inside, and hold the two Germans at gunpoint until help came. In no time I dismissed the idea. Surely Otto was armed with a pistol, just like Derek, and one or the other would shoot. I'd be outnumbered, and if we did have a shootout, Nat and maybe Karl might be killed, and me too.

I had to deal with two important facts: I was outnumbered, 2-1, and my revolver had only six bullets. Not only that but Otto or Derek, or both, might have *more* than one gun.

Suddenly a new thought appeared like a bright light. My best bet would be to sneak down to the outhouse, hide there, and pick off whichever one came to use it first. Several yards away dense trees flanked both sides of the little house. The grass behind it sloped down to the outhouse near the right corner of the back yard, and not too far behind it the ravine began.

I slipped back into the woods, worked my way down to a spot opposite the outhouse, and hid behind a wide oak. From my vantage point I could see everything. The outhouse looked about six feet square, and it was built of old boards. It was unpainted, the slanting roof was covered by tar paper, and a crescent moon was carved in the door. I settled down to think about possibilities.

Several occurred to me. The most likely was that Otto, once he needed to use the outhouse, would not go alone. Since he didn't trust Derek with Nat, he'd probably bring her along but keep her hands tied. I figured if Derek appeared first, he'd be either alone or escorting Karl to the outhouse.

However, if the two men came together and risked leaving the captives alone, I would face the same disadvantage. I'd have to shoot both before either could shoot me, or I was dead. I pulled out my weapon, cocked the hammer, and after a few seconds, I let the hammer down.

The stars above me looked like a mass of dots of lights in a black blanket, and to the east a partial moon was climbing into view like a friend shining a pale light on the forest. From where I stood I could see the back slope. In my hiding place, I practiced aiming the S&W.

Unfortunately, Dad only allowed me to fire six bullets the one time, over a year ago. Mainly he wanted me to understand the danger of using firearms. I remember his words, "If you ever have to shoot, don't hesitate. Fire first. He who hesitates is lost." I knew that was a truism, but I figured Dad knew what he was talking about. I shoved the gun back in my belt.

The last dilemma was if I shot only Otto or Derek, the other one might kill Nat and Karl. To play it safe, I sat down behind the tree to think, but I felt something under my rear end. Standing up, I reached down and found an old chunk of 2x4 beside the oak. My eyes must have sparkled in the dark! My new idea was to use the board to belt the first one to appear.

Moments later I heard a door open, and I looked up. Derek emerged from the back door, and luckily for me, he was alone. Holding a beer bottle in his right hand, he moved unsteadily down the slope with the grass now damp with dew. Stopping a few feet short of the outhouse, he raised the bottle, drained it, and looked toward me like he saw me. In fact, he hurled the bottle at the very tree where I was hiding. His aim wasn't good, because the bottle fell into the ferns close to my feet. He laughed like a hyena, took a step, and opened the outhouse door. Once inside, he banged the wooden door shut, but it bounced part way open.

Derek looked and sounded drunk, so I had an advantage. Dropping the 2x4, I picked up the brownish bottle. The label said *Columbia*. The bottle looked about nine inches long, but the narrow neck formed three inches of it. I could use it like a glass blackjack. Taking a deep breath, I took the bottle and walked carefully toward the outhouse.

Halfway there, I realized Derek might grab the gun from my belt. Turning, I slipped back to the tree, hid the weapon in the ferns, and again crept toward the outhouse, gripping the bottle in my left hand. My toe of my shoe struck something beside the door, and it hurt badly, but I stifled a yell. Moments later, I leaned close to the door, and listened. Inside, I heard Derek moving. Backing up a step, I raised the bottle, yanked open the door, and there was just enough light to see him standing and zipping up his trousers. Startled, he looked up at me, mumbled in German, and tried to buckle his belt. In a flash I swung the bottle hard, breaking it against his forehead. He groaned, and blood spots appeared.

But Derek, stronger than I thought, was only stunned. Quick as a wink he lunged at me, and the force of his weight caused us to fall backwards onto the grass in front of the outhouse. Sputtering in German, he glared at me, gripped my neck, and began strangling me. For a few moments I couldn't breathe, and I felt blackness closing in. The thought of the broken bottle in my hand floated before my eyes like a white light. Mustering my fading strength, I plunged the glass into his neck. Afterward, I remember Derek groaning. His eyes opened wider, turned upward, and blood spurted from the side of his neck. Slowly his fingers slipped off my neck. He gasped a couple of times before rolling off me and flopping over on his back. His eyes stared at the stars he couldn't see. With my breath heaving against my chest, I kept my eyes on him until I felt stronger. Slowly I got to my feet, and I looked up at the silvery moon.

Suddenly I felt like throwing up. Leaning over with my hands on my knees, I braced for the worst. The gag reflex faded, but I was numb, and I stood up and buried my face in my hands. Finally, I took a few deep breaths of mountain air, and I turned to look at the small house above me. Nobody had appeared outside. After a period of watching, waiting, and breathing normally, I glanced down at my shirt. Blood stains had made it a mess, and I was horrified. Suddenly I bent over and lost it. I stayed in that position, hands on knees, for several minutes.

Recovering, I stood upright, moved over, and grabbed Derek's limp hands. I dragged the body quietly past the outhouse and to the edge of the ravine. Dropping his hands, I bent over and pushed him. The body rolled down the ravine about ten or twelve feet, until it was stopped by a large bush. His face was looking in my direction. Anyone looking into the ravine would see the corpse.

Turning away, I thought about cleaning myself up. I pulled off my bloody tee shirt, used the clean back of it to wipe blood off my face, hands, and chest, and I tossed the shirt into the ravine. Not feeling very clean, I leaned over and wiped the palms of my hands on the grass. Again I wiped off my face, and felt better. I looked up at the sky. The stars twinkled as if life below was unchanging. Still, I had journeyed this far to rescue Nat and Karl, and now that meant removing Otto from the picture.

Shirtless, I walked back to the oak tree, felt around in the ferns, and found the revolver. Darkness had become my friend. I moved slowly through the trees, picking my steps carefully, until the lighted window was directly across from me. Leaning forward, I crept across the narrow yard to the wall of the house. Standing next to the window, I peeked again between the half-closed curtains. I could see Nat and Karl tied up in the two chairs at the table. My sister's head was slumped forward like she had dozed off. Karl was looking carefully around like he hoped to find a way to escape. Otto wasn't in sight. While I pondered where he might be, he reappeared with a gun in his right hand. It looked like a military .45 pistol. I knew from watching movies at the theater that such a pistol packed a powerful punch.

Looking his captives over, Otto frowned, and I wondered what he was thinking. For a few minutes he paced around the room. He must have been worried because Derek had not returned. Finally, he sat on the couch, picked up the newspaper, and tried to read. After maybe a minute, he tossed the paper aside, picked up his pistol, and stood up. He walked to a wooden cabinet, took out a flashlight, and smiled. I figured he decided to look for Derek.

The chances of me shooting Otto flashed across my mind. For one thing, I had the advantage of surprise. On the other hand, I had little confidence in being able to shoot him from any distance. I had only fired the pistol on that one occasion, with my father present. I knew Otto's .45 had eight bullets in the magazine. I felt myself sweating, but I was determined to keep moving.

Once more I peeked in, and this time I saw Otto jam the gun in his belt. Moving over, he removed the rope that tied Nat to the chair, but he left her hands bound. He was bringing her with him! Terror tried to rise within me, but in a flash I knew the answer. I would return to the outhouse, because Otto might need to use it. If not, he would doubtless look around the yard to find if something had happened to Derek. Also, Otto would have to check the outhouse, hopefully before he checked the ravine behind it.

Turning, I made my way down the grassy slope, opened the door, and stepped inside. The smell was putrid, but not as bad as I feared. Likely the rundown house was seldom used. I leaned my face close to the door and looked through the crescent-shaped hole. Within a minute Otto appeared, pulling Nat with one hand and sweeping the flashlight back and forth with the other. Slowly they descended the grassy slope with the light glaring ahead like the roving eye of an evil nocturnal animal. Otto said nothing, but I could hear Nat sobbing softly. I pulled out my .38, cocked it, and held the weapon in both hands. I hoped to fire before Otto could draw his gun.

When he and Nat approached within ten feet of me, a loud voice boomed from beside the house: "*Otto Herman! This is the FBI!* You are surrounded! *Drop the weapon, and raise your hands*!"

Reacting quickly, Otto tossed away the flashlight and, using one hand, he jerked Nat in front of him like a human shield.

As I recognized the voice of FBI agent Henry Becker, he yelled, "Let go of Natalia, drop your weapon, and step back. She is going to walk toward us. You are going to lie flat on the ground with your arms ahead of you. *Do it now*!"

I peered through the crack, and I saw two big flashlights trained on Nat and Otto, one shining from each side of the house. I couldn't see Becker, but I knew Dad wasn't far behind him.

Otto kept Nat in front of him, and he raised his weapon to her head. "Not so fast! If there is a gun battle, this little lady goes first. I'll blow her brains out, and we will all lose."

As Nat gasped, Otto waited a few seconds for his words to hit home. "You, sir, will tell all of your men to leave. You will not block the lane. I know you have my friend Derek Miller in custody … So, take off the handcuffs, and let him get into his car. We are driving away together, the three of us, and if you follow or try to head us off, this child gets killed."

It was a stalemate. Nothing was said for maybe half a minute. Now it was a do-or-die crisis. With my S&W cocked, I slowly pushed the outhouse door. I was fortunate, because the door opened without a sound, and Otto didn't hear me. I crept up behind him, raised my revolver toward his head and above the line of her shorter figure.

But just as I pulled the trigger, Otto shifted his position and turned his head, having sensed or heard someone behind him, and instead of penetrating his skull, my bullet missed. Pushing Nat away, he wheeled and turned to face me. We both fired at once, making two loud echoing *bangs*. His slug slammed into my gun arm, knocking the .38 out of my hand and seemingly tearing away a chuck of flesh, but my slug penetrated the left side of his chest. I staggered backward, tripped on something, and fell. Immediately I rolled over, and got to my knees, but I felt too woozy to stand. Looking ahead, I saw Otto a few feet away, also on his knees with his hands spread before him, holding his body up. His advantage was the pistol lay on the ground near his right hand. His disadvantage was he had a slug in his chest doing its cruel damage. The thought flashed across my mind that the bullet hit his lungs because he was gasping for breath while a trickle of blood leaked from the corner of his mouth.

Otto tried to push himself up, but he lacked the strength, and he saw the .45. Grabbing it, he tried to lift his arm and shoot me, but suddenly the gun must have felt too heavy, because he lowered his hand to the grass. I heard footsteps coming down the slope. As my eyes blurred, I saw Nat, her wrists still tied in front of her, come closer, lean over, and pick up the S&W with both hands.

In the dim moonlight I saw Otto's eyes open wider, and he seemed to recognize me. In a whisper he said what I think was "James, my boy …" Rising on his knees, he spread his arms wide as if to embrace me. At the same time Nat clutched our father's .38 revolver, despite her bound wrists.

Turning toward him, she raised the gun while I cleared my throat, hoping to make my words more than legible: "Otto, you are about to die. Go to your grave knowing your almighty Hitler will someday be executed as a war criminal."

Nat squeezed the trigger, and as I struggled to my feet, the S&W spoke its ugly *bang*. The first of the four remaining bullets penetrated Otto's head, exiting through his cheekbone and releasing a tiny gusher of blood. His head jerked forward, but he managed to stay on his knees. Her second shot caused Otto to release the pistol, and the group that was hurrying from the top of the hill stopped in their tracks. Evidently nobody wanted to grab my sister with two bullets left in the weapon. As that thought flashed into my mind, she fired twice more. Slowly the Nazi's body toppled over sideways onto the ground.

Bending over him, Nat squeezed the trigger several times as if to coax another bullet out of the empty chamber. I reached her, pulled the gun slowly out of her trembling hands, and handed it to Dad as Becker watched. Returning his own .45 to its shoulder holster, the agent just looked at us.

Someone cut off the rope around Nat's wrists, and she collapsed in my arms. Neither of us was crying, probably because we were both shell-shocked. Her pale face and white blouse were spattered with drops of blood. Shirtless, I had fresh blood oozing from my left arm. Later, in the car when we were riding home, I asked quietly if she was thinking anything in particular when she fired the four shots. Sighing, she looked straight ahead and recalled, "Otto just laughed when Derek told him with his foul mouth what he planned to do to me when the time came."

Looking at my kid sister, I didn't voice my reply, which was *The time never did come, and it never will.*

CHAPTER 14: Loose Ends

Within the hour the second Ford with FBI agents and local police arrived at the mountain house. Minutes later two more vehicles arrived and parked near the other cars. The first was a white van, and out climbed two men in white uniforms. The second was a black Buick sedan, and the driver wore a gray suit and carried a black medical bag. The pair in white went back to the slope and, carrying flashlights, attended to the dead bodies. The doctor came to us, waiting in front of the house, and opened his bag. Becker held a flashlight while the doctor deftly cleaned the wound in my upper arm. He applied a liquid that stung for several seconds, added a yellow salve that felt smoothing, and bandaged the arm tightly.

Moving to Nat, he smiled and gave her a few quiet words of encouragement. Producing a stethoscope, he listened to her heart, peered into her mouth, asked a couple of questions, and, with a cup of water from his canteen, gave her two aspirins. After making notes in his small notebook, he checked over Karl, who looked exhausted. Afterward, he spoke to Dad and Becker. I heard him say that we were fit for travel, but that all three of us should see a doctor in Charlottesville tomorrow. Looking at us, he observed, "Your arm will heal, but you need to follow the directions I have given to your father."

As he climbed the slope, the white-uniformed men were wrapping the two dead bodies in blue blankets. After they carried the corpses to the van, they returned to collect evidence of the struggle. All the while, agent Russell questioned Nat, although briefly, and Karl, at some length. Following those two, he pulled me aside, questioned me in detail, and took my statement. Afterward, Russell spoke to Becker and left to check inside the house.

I learned that Otto had packed a bag for what he called their "road trip" before he and Derek launched the kidnapping. After Russell finished with us, Karl kindly offered me a shirt. I accepted, happily, I might add. I followed him inside, and we washed up at the sink with its hand pump. Drying myself, I pulled on the blue polo shirt. It was evident that Karl was feeling low due to his uncle involving him in the plot. When I mentioned that point to agent Becker, he spoke to Karl, assuring him that he had no choice in the matter.

By the time Dad had returned with our truck, Becker and Russell had Karl with them in the FBI sedan. Following Nat, I climbed wearily into the pickup. Dad had arranged to take the lead, and the FBI sedan with Russell driving would follow us. As he shifted gears and put the pickup underway, I asked him for the time. Checking his wrist watch, he said 9:35. For the first few minutes, nobody spoke. Nat had a blanket wrapped around her that Becker carried in his trunk for emergencies. She looked warm, but she shivered from time to time. I guessed she had memories that kept flooding back, and I thought better of asking.

But after a few miles under the crescent moon, I spoke to Dad about my last problem. "On the way up here, I stopped at a country store called Elmer's Emporium." He nodded, because they had stopped at the same store. "I got the directions," I added, "just like you later did, from Cecil. He's about my age. Elmer, the owner, is his father, but he wasn't there. When I got the directions, I asked Cecil to give them to you or the FBI or the police. He told me he wanted a 'reward' for helping us."

Dad raised his eyebrows. "A *reward*?"

"Yes, well, I understand that, but I only had $2.75 in my pocket. I gave it to him, but when he said it wasn't much of a reward, I promised to give him the S&W."

Dad looked at me, his blue eyes wide open. "You did? That's not even *your* gun ..."

Holding the steering wheel and focusing on the road ahead, he glanced at my tired face. After a little distance, he observed, "You're right. A promise is a promise, like I always say."

He pulled over to the shoulder, stopped, and set the emergency brake. Climbing out, he walked back to the passenger's side of the black sedan. I turned to look, and by then Becker had climbed out. Dad spoke to the agent, Becker asked a question or two, and I saw the two men nod. Becker climbed back in the Buick, and Dad returned, hoisted himself up into the truck's seat. He shifted gears, and we continued our journey, but with a new intermediate destination. All the time Nat looked at the road ahead and said nothing.

About twenty minutes later we turned into Elmer's Emporium, and a light on the pole by the gas pump was still on. As the black sedan parked beside our truck, two fellows stood up out of old wooden chairs. One was Cecil, and he was wearing the same worn jeans with the same tee shirt. The other was a chunky man in his fifties wearing faded blue bib overalls over a white undershirt. He removed a corn cob pipe from his mouth, and placed it on the arm of the chair.

The three of us climbed out of the pickup, and Becker stepped out of his car. Dad walked over to introduce us, and Nat and I followed. Becker stood near his vehicle's front fender, crossed his arms, and watched. Karl waited beside him. The older man extended his hand to our father.

"Hiya, I'm Elmer. I own the emporium." He swept his hand at the old store. "My son Cecil recognized the black car from when y'all passed through here earlier this evenin'. Course, we ain't seen that truck, but she looks solid, all right. Anyways, we figured y'all would be comin' back this way."

Nat and I shook hands with Elmer, and Cecil smiled broadly. He kept looking at my sister like she was a poster girl. Her cheeks flushed, but I'll admit she looked cute, despite the ordeal.

Dad produced the S&W. "My son James promised your son Cecil that he could have this gun in payment for him giving directions to the FBI, the police, and myself when we passed through here. We may not have reached the cabin without his help. So Cecil came through with his end of the bargain, and now we're here. But I'm afraid I have some bad news."

The black eyes of Elmer and the brown eyes of Cecil homed in on Dad like radar beams. Frowning, Cecil said, "So, you gonna tell us this 'bad news,' or do we gotta guess?"

Dad looked him over. "How old are you, young man?"

Cecil rolled his eyes. "I'm fourteen, iffen it makes any difference. But I can shoot Pop's .35 Remington, and I sure can fire a shotgun, *any* gauge."

Dad smiled. "Since you're underage for using a pistol in Virginia, Cecil, I'll have to give this weapon to your father. I'm sure he'll know what to do."

He handed the S&W over to Elmer, who held it up to the light for a closer look. After a few moments he grinned, showing a couple of missing teeth. He eyed Dad. "Yes sir, this here's a mighty fine gun. Ya know, I got me a cousin down in Roanoke who's got him an S&W. He tells me he can hit one of them dang bull's eyes at one hunert yards." And he winked slowly. "But he's lyin', see?!"

Again Elmer held the revolver up to the light, squinting at it. "I'd say this here gun, it's done seen some action, and it smells like recent. Cain't miss that there gunpowder smell."

"Afraid so," Dad replied. "But we tried to clean it off."

"Waall, don't you fret none." He gave me a crafty look with one eye half closed, like he sensed what had happened. "I'll give it a good goin' over."

Elmer nodded at Dad, the two men shook hands like old friends, and the promise was kept. Again I thanked Cecil. He grinned. "Next time y'all come by the emporium, bud, ya can have all the candy bars ya want!"

We got back into the truck, Becker returned to his sedan, and both engines started. Dad pulled back onto the road, the FBI vehicle followed, and we continued on toward Charlottesville. I mainly looked out the window while Nat talked quietly with Dad as he kept his eyes on the road. I might have dozed, because the next thing I remember, Dad pulled into our driveway followed by Becker's sedan. We all got out of our vehicles, and Dad moved over to shake hands with Becker.

"Mister Baker," the agent said. "I'm satisfied that your son accomplished, in his own manner, the mission I hoped we would be able to complete first. James is a brave young man. Ordinarily, I would not recommend such a course of action, but he and his sister Natalia and their friend Karl Ellis traveled all the way to Richmond to get the agency involved. That was a smart move, and a brave one."

He frowned. "One more thing, sir. The agency would like Karl to stay with your family for a brief time, and we need to have all of you say nothing beyond your home about what happened at that mountain house. The FBI in New York is closing in on the spy net ring as we speak. None of the news agencies have been notified of this secret matter, and if we're fortunate, we can crack the network with no public information ever provided. We want this kidnapping to remain off the record."

As they spoke, Nat turned to me and Karl, and finally she spoke. "You know what got all this started, don't you?" When I shook my head no, she said quietly, "You tell him, Karl."

Karl, who still seemed to be feeling low after the ordeal, nodded slowly. Looking me in the eyes, he said quietly, "When my uncle and Derek took us away that afternoon, it started when my father called Long Distance around lunch. Later, in the car, my uncle turned and glared at me. 'So, nephew, your father asked me today what I thought of your, and I quote, *fluency in German*. You tricked me into believing you did not understand my private conversations with Derek.' He gave me the evil eye, and added, 'So, it's your own fault you were kidnapped.'"

I sighed. "I don't think so, Karl. That pair planned to extort secret information from your father by kidnapping you. Nat just happened to be working there, so they took her, too." I shook my head. "So, it really wasn't your fault. It just changed the *timing* of what they planned when your dad called."

His eyes said he understood, and we looked at Dad and Becker. Becker was hoping our father would agree to keep the entire business off the record, and, of course, he agreed. The two men acknowledged the promise with a handshake, and the agent indicated he would return.

Becker climbed back into his car, Russell started the engine, and the sedan backed out of the driveway. We trooped inside the house after what was the most dangerous day of my life and, I'm sure, the most harrowing of Nat's life. Karl still looked out of sorts, even after I let him know he wasn't responsible. I guess he was beating himself up inside, maybe for getting Nat involved.

Despite the late hour, Aunt Cora was waiting in the kitchen. She greeted us with hugs, even for Karl. Indeed, Cora hugged Nat as tight as a vice. Backing away, she looked at all of us for a long minute. Plopping down in a kitchen chair, Cora covered her face with her hands and bawled. Nat sat next to her, put her arm around her shoulders, and in no time she was crying too. I looked at our father, and he was watching them cry. Soon I saw a few tears roll down his cheeks.

"Dad, I'm going upstairs to bed. I'm just wiped out by all that's happened today."

He eyed me. "I thought you might want to talk about it. I'm not blaming you for going off to search for Otto and Derek and, of course, for Nat and Karl. You did what you believed you needed to do. If that had ever happened to me and your mother, I would have done the same."

I grinned. "Thanks, Dad. But I really am tired. Can it wait for tomorrow?"

He indicated it could, and turning to Karl, he said, "I'll get a blanket and a pillow, but you can sleep on our davenport for tonight."

Karl managed a weak smile, but I saw tears in his eyes as I left to drag myself upstairs to the sanctuary of my bedroom. To tell the truth, I was happy to be alive. I flopped down on my bed with clothes on, and relaxed. For a while I stared at the ceiling reflecting on the day's events. After some time my mind turned to playing ball. I was looking forward to the next game. After all, playing baseball is mainly what summer's about.

The last thing I remember that night was my vision of going up to bat with the bases loaded, the crowd cheering like crazy, and Nat's voice yelling, "*Hit it, James! Hit it*! And a big curve floated to the plate, and I swung the bat as hard as I could, and I flew after the ball into a fluffy cloud.

II

The next morning I came downstairs at 7:45. I knew Karl had slept on our mohair davenport, and he was sitting in one chair at the kitchen table. He smiled awkwardly at me. Aunt Cora was whipping up a big breakfast with the help of Nat, who kept sneaking peeks at Karl. He kept moving his eyes from the doorway to Nat, and back. Grinning, I greeted everyone. At that moment Dad came inside, wiping his forehead. As usual, he had begun his work early.He sat next to Karl, and looked at his sister-in-law. "Are we about ready to eat?"

Aunt Cora and Nat smiled at each other, and I think we enjoyed the best breakfast ever. The whole day went smoothly, and Karl helped me with the chores. I think he felt relieved to have something useful to do. Nat helped Aunt Cora with cleaning the house. Everyone seemed to be feeling good, even though I knew Nat and Karl had to digest their ugly memories, related but different from my bad memories.

That night Dad prepared the bed in the small spare bedroom, and he told Karl he was welcome to sleep there rather than on the couch. Karl agreed, and his expression indicated relief. But when Dad opened the bedroom for Karl, I quickly conceived a plan. I realized Nat had spent most of our first afternoon at home taking a walk with Karl to the back of our land where they spent some time on the bench under the big oak. I knew they had plenty to commiserate about, but I also knew they had feelings for each other, and I didn't want him to take advantage of her. So I resolved to leave my bedroom door open at night, not my normal habit. That way if one of them walked toward the other's bedroom, I would hear the footsteps, appear in the hall, and prevent any late night romancing.

A couple of days passed as we returned to normal. Karl proved quite useful helping around the farm, and I played a baseball game with the Broncos on Monday afternoon. Walt Bunker and Jack Jones in particular kept asking me about the guy named Karl who was staying at our house. Finally, I said, "Karl's one of our father's relatives, and he's visiting us for a while."

I tried my best to concentrate on the game, but it was tough. In the end, following two earlier strikeouts and a popup to third base, I came up with nobody out in the seventh, Walt at second, and Mike Houchins, a sophomore, at first. Luke Williams, a slender right-handed freshman with good breaking pitches, tried to strike me out on curve balls. But he was tiring and his control was slipping by the last inning. Once at the plate, I resolved to take one strike before swinging. Williams caught me with a quick fastball on the first pitch, but he missed outside on his first two curves, so the count went to 2-1. I swung a bit high on the next curve, topping one that rolled foul past third. The next two pitches were slow curves that broke low and away, and I walked.

I felt relieved as I trotted down to first, and my walk moved up the runners and loaded the bases. Up came Adam Zimmerman, who had surprised everyone in the first game with his home run. All the moms and dads and friends in the bleachers were on their feet, and several chanted phrases like "Go Adam!" and "Hit another homer!"

Taking a lead, I looked in at Adam ready to hit. I could see he was nervous, but he's smart. Sure enough, he came through. He laid down a perfect bunt, rolling the ball slowly toward first, and he flew down the line like a scared jackrabbit! Walt had taken a big lead at third, and he took off for home plate just as Adam squared to bunt. Walt's heads-up hustle allowed him to score standing up, and the throw from Scott Matthews, the first baseman, got there a second late. But Scott is a good sport, and after the run scored, he gave Adam the credit. All of our guys were milling around and slapping the "slugger" on the back. Adam took a lot of kidding about his "long hit," but it was all in fun as we earned our second win, 6-5. I don't think anyone was happier than Coach Spencer and Adell, who had the red cooler full of Coca-Colas.

After the game ended, we exchanged comments with the guys on the other team. I packed my duffel bag and laughed at the jokes of our teammates. Then we listened as the coach yelled instructions about our next game. A while later Walt and I left to walk home, and on the way we talked about the summer ahead. After a while we got to talking about girls. I told him about Linda Lawton, and he told me about Claudia Rogers.

Once Walt started talking, it all came tumbling out like I'd pulled a plug on his secrets. "Claudia is really nice, and she's cute. And we ran into each other at the movies one Saturday."

"C'mon! You *ran into* her?" It was my turn to smile, and I did.

His cheeks turned red. "Well … anyway, she's got brown hair like Linda's, maybe not as long, but Claudia has those big hazel eyes. It's like she sees *everything*, you know? And she dresses real nice. Overall, I'd say she just *looks good*."

I nodded, we kept walking, and Walt kept talking: "She's real smart, and like a bookworm. You always see her in the library during study hall. I think she's a library assistant, or whatever they call the helpers shelving books, and that stuff. They say she's a 'teacher's pet' in Bronston's Social Studies. I think that means she answers questions, and doesn't whisper with her friends."

By that time we reached his house, and I had an idea. "Walt, look, why don't we plan to go on a *double date*, you know, to the first dance after a home football game?"

Walt gave me his slick smile. "Think, James. Why don't we ask them to go to the *game* together, too, buddy?"

He gave me this huge smile, and I'm wondering, *Why didn't I think of that?*

"*WALT*! Come on, Walt!"

It was his Mom yelling from the front porch. We looked at each other, and he said, "Let's keep this double date idea a secret between us. Later, like in August, we can get together one evening, maybe at your house, and you call Linda, and I'll call Claudia."

Walt's smile was really wide, and we shook hands. Wheeling around, he ran like a scalded dog along the driveway. After watching him for a moment, I headed for home whistling "Zip-a-Dee-Doo-Dah."

At home our lives moved ahead smoothly for a couple more days. Oddly, I felt myself disliking Karl, but I never did mention it. He seemed nice enough, but I felt like he was paying too much attention to my sister. Reflecting on my attitude, I decided the smart thing to do was play it safe and wait and see what resulted.

Nearly a week after we returned home, I woke up and looked at my alarm clock. It said 7:15. I looked at my half-open window. To my surprise a robin had landed on the ledge. When he *chirred*, I figured he was scolding me for sleeping late. I hopped up, pulled on a green polo shirt, a clean pair of jeans, and my brown shoes. After combing my hair, I hurried down to the kitchen. Aunt Cora and Nat were making breakfast, and Karl and Dad were sitting at the kitchen table and chatting about the farm and the summer. Karl was telling him a little about the kidnapping, but they dropped the subject when I arrived.

Half an hour later, after finishing breakfast, we heard a car pull into the driveway. Dad and I hurried into the living room and looked out a front window. Agent Henry Becker was climbing out of a long black Ford, and he had another man with him. Aunt Cora, Nat, and Karl joined us, and we stepped out on the porch.

Smiling, Dad descended the steps, joined Becker, and they shook hands. Karl hurried down the stairs and hugged the stranger. Grinning, Becker introduced Karl's father, Lionel Ellis. A couple of inches shorter than his son's six feet, Mister Ellis had blue eyes, blond hair, and a thin face that looked worried. Dad invited everyone inside, and we walked into the living room. Everyone was smiling, and Karl's father stepped forward.

"It seems we have a great deal to thank you for," he said to me, and tears formed in his eyes. Pulling out a handkerchief, he looked embarrassed. He dabbed at the tears, and smiled again. Aunt Cora recognized the awkward situation for Mister Ellis and Karl, and she asked, "Lemonade, anyone?"

Everyone took seats around the kitchen table, Nat sat beside Karl, and Aunt Cora poured tall glasses of fresh lemonade. A few remarks were exchanged until finally Becker got everyone's attention. "Mainly we're here to let you know the New York end of the spy ring has been smashed. The man called Comrade X, whom it turns out is Wolfgang Schmidt from Berlin and a former member of the Wehrmacht, is behind bars along with all of his accomplices. Mister Ellis here is safe, and, as you know, Otto Herman and his accomplice Derek Miller have both been eliminated."

He took a swig of lemonade. "It turns out that Herman, who's real name was Herman Renken, had been active in the German American Bund since 1938. A well-educated man, he wrote anti-Semitic pamphlets and related articles for private distribution to like-minded Americans, that is, Americans who secretly favored Hitler and the Nazis. The scraps of paper that rained down on your farm after the explosion at the Herman house were surely written by Renken. In the rubble, we found a half-melted mimeograph machine that he would have used to make multiple copies of documents. He was paid by a rich American fascist, and he never was a farmer."

As he enlightened us about Otto, Aunt Cora's face slowly turned red. Tears appeared in her eyes, but Becker said, "Missus Raleigh, you had no way of knowing the man's real identity. And your brother-in-law and his son have both stated for the record that you offered vital clues to the whereabouts of the mountain house." He smiled broadly. "Ma'am, we are thanking you too."

Becker's explanation and his smooth touch with Aunt Cora made our day. Dad was blinking away tears while the Richmond agent spoke to our favorite aunt. I was deeply impressed, and I could see Nat and Karl felt good about the outcome.

When Becker finished, Aunt Cora stood up and said, "I will make all of you a very good lunch." She turned to Nat. "And Nat and her friend Karl are going to help, aren't you?"

They were both grinning. I knew Aunt Cora had in mind keeping an eye on that personal situation. Before she could say any more, Becker stood up too. "I didn't get a chance to say so, but Mister Ellis as well as Karl will be driving with me to Richmond this afternoon. The agency has made airplane reservations for them to fly to New York tomorrow, and …"

He withdrew two tickets from his suit coat and checked them. "Yes, their flight departs at 8:10 am."

That put a whole new light on my worries about my sister. Even as I was relieved from what proved to be pointless concerns, Dad got to his feet, smiling. "May I ask a question?"

Becker nodded. "Who gets the farm owned by our late Mister Herman, however we address him?"

Lionel looked at our father. "We knew him for years as Otto Herman, so I'll use that name. Otto's late wife was my sister, but when all of the legalities are completed, I believe I'm his closest living relative, at least in this country. But as you know, I'm a research chemist. I have no interest in farming, or indeed, leaving New York City."

Satisfied, he looked at everyone in turn. Wasting no time, Dad said, "Well, I would like you to consider this. At the right time I will make you a fair offer to buy that land. I'd like to expand with a herd of beef cattle, and I don't have enough acreage."

Mister Ellis looked at Karl, who quickly nodded. "Well, Zeke Baker, the father whose son saved my son's life, if and when the farm comes into our hands, I will gladly sell it to you, but at a discount." He arose, walked around the table, and the two shook hands. Smiling, Karl's father said, "Yes, sir, you have my word on it."

While Aunt Cora, Nat, and Karl proceeded to prepare a big lunch, Dad offered to show agent Becker and Mister Ellis around our farm. "I know you're city slickers, but I'll give you an idea of why I love living in the country on a farm near Charlottesville, Virginia!"

Everyone enjoyed a good laugh after Dad's remark, a long walk followed, and then we ate a big lunch. Afterward, we all stood up, and the final conversations proceeded on a high note. Later, outside next to the FBI vehicle, Nat and Karl hugged each other and promised to write. Along with Dad, I shook hands with agent Henry Becker, chemist Lionel Ellis, and his loyal son. I could tell from the final goodbyes that a unique bond had developed between myself, my sister, and Karl, based on our shared adventures as teenage spies.

POSTSCRIPT

You have just read a narrative I wrote in the summer of '43 when I was sixteen. I was writing as much as I could remember about the wartime adventure my sister Natalia and I experienced the year before, early in the summer of 1942. Recently I came across the typed pages that my father had stored in a trunk along with some of my clothes, books, pictures, and other mementos of our earlier years.

I read the pages for the first time since I had put them away before leaving for college. Now that the story will be published as a book, I tweaked the manuscript in several places. But I resisted the temptation to revise it considerably to fit into our modern era. Today I would write the story differently, but I doubt if the resulting manuscript would capture the times better than the words of my inexperienced voice.

Still, a fellow writer who read this manuscript commented on how the story really evolves. He said it begins like an adventure of the Bobbsey Twins or the Hardy Boys, but turns tense and suspenseful like something out of Hitchcock, and ends with a dash of violence worthy of today's Hollywood directors. Regardless, ignoring the embarrassment of having my amateur work mentioned in the same breath with professional writers, the comment is essentially correct. This book begins as a teenage spy story but it ends as something else entirely. In every sentence I wrote, my youthful self was telling the tale as faithfully I remembered it.

The history of the Manhattan Project along with the work done later at Los Alamos in the creation of the first atomic bomb is not only well known but has been written about extensively. It is also part of the historical record that the Germans attempted to create an atomic weapon of their own, but in the end they fell short, fortunately for the rest of the world. The juvenile curiosity of me and my sister as teenage spies, which eventually grew into an experience that thwarted the attempt of a network of Nazis to penetrate the Manhattan Project, has not received even a footnote in history. But this narrative is not an attempt to "set the record straight," not the least because there is no documentation to back it up. Therefore, I think readers should understand this tale as fiction, and enjoy it like any other mystery novel.

Federal agent Henry Becker became one of my lifelong heroes. He was the FBI personified, and without his assistance, we may never have been able to rescue Nat and Karl and help crack the far-flung ring of Nazi agents.

Later, when I attended college, I considered a career with the FBI. In the end, I decided to become a history professor and teach American History. Years passed, and I devoted a good deal of time and thought to researching and writing historical articles. Later, I wrote some baseball books, and, even later, several mystery novels. I also read countless mysteries. One of my favorite authors is Ross MacDonald and his protagonist, Lew Archer.

Last but not least, I always kept in close touch with my sister. We were siblings and remain lifelong friends. I smile whenever I reflect on how being teenage spies and helping the war effort started one fine day when Nat and I took bags of potatoes to the farm of our neighbor, whom we soon discovered to be a secret Nazi agent. As a result, my sister convinced me to get involved in spying. Otherwise, our lives would have been considerably different and likely nowhere near as gratifying.

Also from Our Family Press...

Thank you for reading *Teen Spies*—a story sparked by three generations of imagination, creativity, and love.

The adventure doesn't end here...

Coming Soon: *Teen Targets*
The thrilling sequel that takes our young heroes deeper into danger—and closer to the truth.

Stay up to date with all of our family-published books, bonus content, and special releases at:

https://www.jimsargentbooks.com/

- Explore more titles by our authors

- Get behind-the-scenes peeks and early sneak previews

- Sign up for exclusive reader updates and offers

Thank you for being part of our story. See you in the next mission.

www.ingramcontent.com/pod-product-compliance
Lightning Source LLC
Chambersburg PA
CBHW071525100726
47908CB00004B/1291